ADVENTURES

W9-AVT-345

READ ALL THE

ADVENTURES

BOOK 1: THE SECRET OF STONESHIP WOODS

BOOK 2: THE MASSIVELY MULTIPLAYER MYSTERY

BOOK 3: THE QUANTUM QUANDARY

BOOK 4: THE DOOMSDAY DUST

BOOK 5: THE SHRIEKING SHADOW

BOOK 6: THE OMEGA OPERATIVE

THE OMEGA OPERATIVE

BY RICK BARBA

ALADDIN PAPERBACKS
New York London Toronto Sydney

This book is a work of fiction. Any references to historical
events, real people, or real locales are used fictitiously. Other
names, characters, places, and incidents are the product of
the author's imagination, and any resemblance to actual events
or locales or persons, living or dead, is entirely coincidental.

ALADDIN PAPERBACKS
An imprint of Simon & Schuster Children's Publishing Division
1230 Avenue of the Americas, New York, NY 10020
Text copyright © 2007 by Wild Planet Entertainment, Inc.
Illustrations copyright © 2006 by Scott M. Fischer
Map of Carrolton copyright © 2006 by Eve Steccati
All rights reserved. Spy Gear and Wild Planet trademarks are the
property of Wild Planet Entertainment, Inc. San Francisco, CA 94104
All rights reserved, including the right of
reproduction in whole or in part in any form.
ALADDIN PAPERBACKS and related logo are
registered trademarks of Simon & Schuster, Inc.
Designed by Tom Daly
The text of this book was set in Weiss.
Manufactured in the United States of America
First Aladdin Paperbacks edition August 2007
2 4 6 8 10 9 7 5 3 1
Library of Congress Control Number 2007926175
ISBN-13: 978-1-4169-0892-0
ISBN-10: 1-4169-0892-7

CONTENTS

1   FRIGHTENING THINGS WITH CLAWS AND
    TENTACLES AND CHEWING MOUTHPARTS   1

2   THE KID   13

3   OLD ACQUAINTANCES   26

4   ODD HOUSE   40

5   DOGS, BUGS, AND SQUIDS   56

6   THE FELLOWSHIP OF THE WHATEVER   69

7   DOCTOR WHO?   81

8   HUNTER   98

9   HAVING A BALL   115

10 CHUTES AND LADDERS   129

11 A GIRL POSSESSED   138

12 BACK IN THE SADDLE   151

13 VIPER AT LAST   162

14 THE FINAL CHAPTER   173

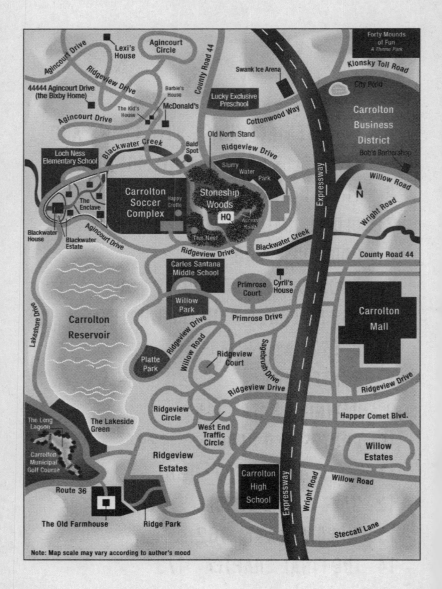

Note: Map scale may vary according to auther's mood

TEAM SPY GEAR

 JAKE BIXBY

 LUCAS BIXBY

 CYRIL WONG

 LEXI LOPEZ

FRIGHTENING THINGS WITH CLAWS AND TENTACLES AND CHEWING MOUTHPARTS

Now that I got your attention with that *ridiculous* chapter title, let's get right down to business, shall we? Something's going on down there. It looks suspicious. Let's check it out!

See that small convoy of Russian-made KAMAZ-535 military transport trucks?

No, not the one in Tajikistan. You've panned too far east again. You guys are always panning too far east. Come on, people! Let's get those KH-12 spy satellites under control. Those trucks in Tajikistan are just practicing for their impending invasion of England. We don't care about that. Pan *west!*

There, *that* convoy:

The one rumbling up the high pass in the eastern mountains of Uzbekistan.

The road is very dry, so the big Russian trucks kick up a lot of dust.[1] Dust is everywhere. I can't see clearly, even though my spy telescope is so incredibly powerful. I need a better viewing angle. I'd really like to pilot the International Space Station just a little bit to the left, but that's hard to do when you're hiding in a closet.[2]

So you're asking, *What's so suspicious about a bunch of trucks driving through a mountain pass in Uzbekistan?* To that, I would answer, *Nothing . . . at first glance.* And so you'd take a second glance, maybe even a third, and then say, *You know, Mr. Barba, I still don't see anything particularly suspicious.* At that point I would accidentally hit the Off button to cut off the radio transmission.

Wait. There it is.

The trucks are stopping. Two men jump out of the cab in the lead vehicle.

They walk up to a solid granite rock face rising up on the left side of the road. As they approach, a section of the rock tilts upward, revealing a cave opening large enough for, say, a convoy of trucks to enter, one by one. The two men return to the lead vehicle and the convoy of trucks enters, one by one.

---

1. Big Russian trucks are designed to kick up a lot of dust even when it isn't dusty. Kids, this is the kind of secret fact you learn from watching Hollywood movies.

2. If the astronauts find me, they'll beat me up . . . which, in zero gravity, might be kind of fun, now that I think of it.

As the last truck enters the side of the cliff wall, it grinds to a sudden halt. We see the rear flap of the truck flutter a bit.

Now the driver appears. He walks around to the back of the truck and crouches to examine something under the rear gate.

Then, suddenly, something thrusts through the flap.

It looks like a pair of giant claws—the claws of, say, a praying mantis.

Quick as lightning, these claws snatch the man into the back of the big Russian truck.

Okay, now . . . *that* was creepy.

We'd better go report this to the Bixbys, eh, fellow spies?

First, swivel left. Stick your arms straight out like Superman and then rocket at Mach 17 around the gentle blue curve of the planet.[3] When you see North America, pitch downward and re-enter the atmosphere so you can breathe again, unless you're already dead, in which case you'll just have to keep orbiting. As you descend, the air pressure really builds, so try not to explode.

Okay, you're doing really well.

Now aim for the middle of the continent.

Wow, it's summertime there. Very hot and humid.

3. If your face starts to melt, you might want to slow down a bit.

Very unpleasant. Really, if Iberian monkeys hadn't invented air conditioning during the last ice age, I think we'd all be in trouble, especially because of the monkey smell.

Aha! Look down there. That's Carrolton, where the Bixby brothers live.

Keep diving. It's getting hotter, isn't it?

That's because summer in Carrolton was invented by guys who planned to use the entire city to bake bread. But then people moved in, homesteaders and whatnot. This of course was back in the 1400s, when people were stupid and had only one arm. Kids, I highly recommend that you read history books about those early days of our nation. You'll laugh so hard!

Anyway, as you tumble screaming toward Carrolton, veer toward the north end of town.

See all those blue pools surrounded by white twisty tubes? That's Carrolton's summer fun place, the Slurry Water Park. Here, kids don swimsuits and spend all day standing in line, waiting hours in order to plummet fifteen seconds down a slide that will haunt them with horrifying nightmares for the rest of their conscious lives. It's just so much fun! On a really hot day, like today for example, you get the added benefit of painful third-degree burns on the bottom of your bare feet. We recommend that you wear sandals around the park, although you should take them off really quick if they start to melt or smoke.

Anyway, we point out Slurry Water Park because something very strange is happening at the park today. The walkways are deserted right now, because the front gates don't open for another twenty minutes.

Look over there, at the "Gruesome Dinosaurs of Hideous Death!" ride.

It consists of a series of dark caverns filled with shrieking, poorly lit meat-eaters. These caverns are connected by vertical tubes. You get into an inflated raft with two or three other passengers, float into the ride's entrance tunnel, and then drop straight down three miles into the Earth's core.

Very few kids know what actually happens during the ride itself. Most people pass out during the first fall and don't wake up until the end, when you finally emerge from the exit tunnel into daylight, your raft drenched with blood and fish guts.

It's easily the most popular ride in the water park, as you can well imagine.

But wait . . . *did you see that?*

There? Near the ride entrance?

Wow!

Something rather large and black just crawled out of the bushes and slipped into the water. There! See it? It's swimming into the dinosaur ride!

Wow!

It looks like a big black starfish with extra-long arms!

Wow!

Wow!

Settle down, will you?

Okay, the ground is coming up pretty fast now. Better veer south a bit.

Hey! That's Cyril Wong's hair!

It's walking down the street with Lexi Lopez!

Those are, like, two of our favorite things. And here's an added bonus: The rest of Cyril is directly beneath his hair!

This is extraordinarily good luck.

Two other kids, both strangers, troop along beside Cyril and Lexi. These two strangers look and act like brothers, but they can't be, because it's Tuesday. On Tuesday, of course, brothers are banned. Or wait, maybe I'm thinking of Carrolton's Tuesday ban on downtown parking, where parking is banned, not brothers. So maybe those two boys *are* brothers. Maybe not. There's only one way to find out.

As you slam into the ground next to them at about 600 mph, notice how they talk to each other.

Let's listen in, shall we?

Tromping along, Cyril glances around at the surrounding neighborhood lawns.

Why are all these people slamming into the ground from outer space? he wonders. But he says nothing about it. Instead, he turns to one of the two strangers, the older one, and says, "Jake, I've been thinking."

"Uh-oh," answers the tall strange boy.

"No, don't worry, dude, this time it has nothing to do with hair or hair-related issues or hair products," Cyril reassures him.

The smaller of the two strange boys gives his possible big brother a look.

"It has something to do with Stoneship Woods, I'll wager," says the small strange boy. "Or my name isn't Lucas Bixby."

Strong statement. But who are these strange boys? Maybe we can get a clue from Lexi, who whips forward into a few quick cartwheels as she moves along.

"I think . . . it's time . . . we went . . . back in," she says, cartwheeling.

Cyril stares at her. "Is that right?" he says.

"Yes," says Lexi.

"Why?"

"Because it's time," she replies.

Cyril nods. "I see your logic there," he says with a thoughtful rub of his chin. "But no, that's not what I was thinking about. It was something else entirely."

Lexi does a couple of spin moves, then bows. She's in a great mood today. "Well, I think we should all go into the woods, climb some trees, and spy," she says with a bright smile. "And I should be leader."

Cyril looks at the two strangers. "Well, Bixbys, what say ye to this nonsense?"

"Hear, hear," says the taller unknown character with a killer grin. "Agreed, Lucas?"

"I'm all for it, Jake," says the smaller fellow whose identity or name nobody can figure out. "I think Team Spy Gear has given the Agency plenty of time to solve things on their own." He nods at Lexi. "But, guys, you can only give adults so much time before you should step in and clean up their mess."

Cyril scoffs. "That's just the sort of thing I'd expect Lucas Bixby to say to his older brother Jake Bixby," scoffs Cyril. Scoffing, he adds, "I'm opposed to this violation of the woods ban, myself."

"Of course you are," says the stranger who seems to be a younger brother of some sort.

Stoneship Woods is the spooky forest in the center of Carrolton. Everybody knows that. But you may not know that at the end of the last book in this gripping adventure series—that would be Book 5: *The Shrieking Shadow*—a shadowy government spy agency known as the Agency shut down access to Stoneship Woods because of certain creepy activities there. Local "health authorities" sealed off Stoneship's perimeter with yellow CAUTION! tape and posted scary warning signs claiming that mosquitoes carrying West Nile virus have infested the area. These authorities also set up a series of checkpoints on the surrounding roads and installed a network of motion detector alarms along the dark forest's perimeter.

Doesn't that seem like an awfully sophisticated quarantine for a simple mosquito infestation? And the beefy dudes in orange reflector vests who man the checkpoints 24/7 look more like Special Forces recon units than Health Department employees.

This is all laughable because, as every kid in Carrolton knows, far grislier things lurk in Stoneship Woods than a few diseased mosquitoes. Plus nobody ever goes in there anyway.

Except Team Spy Gear, of course.

"I don't like fear, Jake," says Cyril. "In fact, I fear it. And I find it frightening." He sighs. "Plus, I don't see how we could get past all the 'Health Department' checkpoints, unless we master invisibility."

"Actually, invisible kids would set off the motion detector alarms they've installed around the perimeter," says the older stranger. "So, dude, what is it you've been thinking about?"

"Oh, right," says Cyril, remembering. "I've been thinking about high school, actually."

"What about it?"

"Like, is it possible to attend Carrolton High School from afar?" asks Cyril.

"How far?"

"I'm thinking, like, Indonesia."

Lexi hoots like an insane owl. "You're afraid of getting beat up by senior football players, aren't you?" she says.

"That's part of it," admits Cyril.

"What's the other part?"

"Decay," says Cyril.

"Decay?" repeats the older stranger.

"Yes, decay," says Cyril. "Nobody really keeps an eye on it, except me. But if I have to go to high school every day, well . . . *anything could happen.*"

Lexi and the two strangers crack up.

Okay, well then, let's move on, shall we?

We really need to find the Bixbys, or else this story can't go much further.

Hold on just a second, though.

Before we find those elusive Bixbys, let's take one last quick look at Uzbekistan.

There. Those two men in the cave—one tall man, one short.

They stagger down a dank underground passage. The taller visitor shines a halogen flashlight ahead. His shorter companion stumbles once, but steadies himself on the wet, slimy rock wall. They follow a trail of red reflector strips along the floor.

Seconds later they emerge into an open cavern—a large space filled with echoes. Just ahead, a man in a metal chair is bent so far forward that his head rests on his knees. His arms hang limply. Long gray hair spills from his head over his legs.

Next to him, a very large figure is draped in a pale hooded cape.

The two visitors bow to the caped figure. Suddenly, the man in the chair sits bolt upright. In the dim reddish light, his eyes appear to be jet-black.

The two visitors drop to their knees in fright. Both lower their heads, afraid to look.

"Is the landing site ready?" hisses the man.

"Yes," says the tall visitor.

The black-eyed man in the chair moves his head in odd, jerking motions. Then he says, "The Agency is still fully focused on the nest colony?"

"Yes," says the tall visitor.

"Good," says the man. And his head abruptly drops to his knees again.

There is a brief silence.

The two kneeling visitors venture a glance up . . . just in time to see a thick black fluid gushing from the man's nose, ears, and mouth as he gags and coughs violently. The oily fluid splashes to the cave floor. Then the black puddle gathers—yes, *gathers*—and slowly seeps under the cape of the great hooded figure.

The two visitors, eyes wide, watch in rigid fear.

The man in the chair gasps loudly, and sits up again.

This time his eyes look normal, if somewhat distressed and bloodshot. Next to him, the massive, hooded figure shudders once . . . and begins to stir.

Two huge armlike protrusions push forward beneath the cape's gray fabric. Then, with a sudden snap, the cloak is whipped backward.

Its hood falls.

The visitors scream.

And yes, so does the author.

2

THE KID

I guess I just can't fool you people.

Apparently, you knew all along that those two fellows with Cyril and Lexi are indeed the Bixby brothers. Well done!

But enough tomfoolery. Let's get right down to business.

Like I said earlier, it's summertime. Aside from Christmas, there's just no better time of year for a kid than summertime, unless you live in the Mojave Desert where it's so hot that fire actually melts. Of course, like many well-meaning but horribly misguided parents, Carrolton parents try their hardest to *ruin* summer for kids.

For example, the City of Carrolton offers tons of "organized summer activities" (*ugh!*): art camp, science camp, band camp, computer camp, soccer camp, insect camp, zoo camp, horse camp, asparagus camp, and butt-chomping camp. (I'm not sure what you do in some of these camps, and frankly, I don't want to know.) But what kids *really* need during summer is plenty of what I like to call "nothing camp"—yes, a camp where you do nothing. Doing nothing is actually good for kids. In fact, sometimes nothing is *far* better than something. Especially in the summertime.

Right now, for example, Team Spy Gear is walking down the street. That's it. That's all there is to the story. Just walking. They're approaching Willow Park, where they might hang around or not, or else they might, or they might not. As you heard earlier, they're also thinking about sneaking into Stoneship Woods, maybe, which is not far from Willow Park.

They're in the process of deciding right now. Let's listen in again, shall we?

Cyril scratches his hair. "Man, something itches on my scalp," he says.

"Uh-oh," says Jake.

Many cosmic forces are at work within the orbit of Cyril's hair. For example, it has its own gravity well. But then he reaches in and finds some forks and a big spoon. He looks at these utensils.

"Huh," he says.

"Dude, that's a *soup* ladle," says Lucas, impressed.

"How did those get in your hair?" asks Lexi.

"That's actually none of your business," says Cyril.

14

Lexi cracks up.

Lucas nods toward the Willow Park playground, just ahead. "Hey, I've got an idea," he blurts out.

"Sweet!" exclaims Lexi.

Lexi is a big fan of Lucas Bixby Ideas. They're always unusual. For example, once Lucas devised a plan to reverse time. It didn't work, but everyone had a lot of fun with the magnets.

"I think I can rig up that twisty slide in the playground so that when you slide down, you undergo molecular restructuring," he says. "Your protons will get shocked into a unipolar orientation, creating what I suspect will be a wormhole to an alternate universe."

"Will there be unicorns there?" asks Lexi.

"Probably," says Lucas, nodding professionally.

Cyril gasps. "Then count me out!" he says.

Lexi stares at him. "You're scared of unicorns?" she asks.

"Only the disease," says Cyril.

"What disease?" asks Lexi defensively. She loves unicorns.

"It's too complicated," says Cyril.

"What disease?" repeats Lexi.

"You're too little to understand."

Lexi socks Cyril in the stomach. All of his guts fly out and it takes everyone about ten minutes to stuff them back in.

"Whew!" says Cyril. "That was fun!"

Anyway, do you see what I mean about summer? Plans can change at the drop of a hat. It's beautiful, man. Just twenty minutes ago, Team Spy Gear originally assembled on the porch of the Bixby house at 44444 Agincourt Drive to have a Frisbee war in the backyard. But that plan changed. The new plan: Use a stopwatch to precisely time the long walk from the Bixby house to Cyril's house and then on down to Carrolton High School.

Why?

Because last spring, not long after the hair-raising events described so profoundly and deepfully[4] in Book 5 of this series, *The Shrieking Shadow*, Cyril and Jake graduated from eighth grade at Carlos Santana Middle School. Come this September, they'll be *high school freshmen!* Yes, it's shocking and sad. But kids, time moves on. Children (even you) grow up. Pet goldfish die. Book series end. You'd better enjoy stuff while you can. Enjoy everything . . . every minute of it!

Except for school lunches.

Please don't enjoy those.

Anyway, next year Jake plans to walk to Carrolton High School on good weather days even though his mother, Mrs. Bixby, has offered to drive him every morning unless she's sick, in which case she'll deploy an AH-64

---

4. I like this word. That's why I made it up.

Apache gunship escort. But Jake Bixby is getting older. He wants to do stuff "by himself" (which means "without his mother") . . . stuff like, say, going to high school. His planned walking route runs to Cyril's house first; there, Cyril will join Jake for the next leg of the trek. Being typical guys, Jake and Cyril want to know the latest possible moment they can sleep and still make it to school by first bell. Hence the stopwatch.

But then that plan got tossed out because somebody "changed their mind," which is an *amazing* power, boys and girls.

Now Willow Park is the team's destination.

"Anybody want a fork?" asks Cyril, holding up forks. "I need to get rid of these."

Jake grins. He's about to make a comment about Cyril's eating habits when something catches his eye. A kid in black pants, black sneakers, and a black hooded sweatshirt leans against a lamppost near the bus stop just up the street. The hood is pulled up over his head, hiding his face.

"There he is again," says Jake.

"Who?" asks Lucas, looking around.

"Where?" asks Lexi.

"And don't forget *When?* and *What?*" adds Cyril. "Those are my personal favorites."

Before the others can spot him, the hooded kid slinks into a nearby sprouting of new trees.

"He just ducked into those little trees behind the bus stop," says Jake, halting. "See him?"

Cyril moves up next to his buddy. "Yes, and why do we care?" he asks.

"He's been hanging around," says Jake.

"Around where?"

Jake shrugs. "All over."

Cyril looks over at Lucas and Lexi and asks, "Have *you* seen this kid?"

"No," says Lucas.

"No," says Lexi.

"No," says the red rooster.

"Jake," says Cyril. "We all agree. Apparently, you're insane."

"Dude, I've seen him, like, five or six times in the past week," insists Jake. "It seems like every time I turn around, he's there."

Cyril spins around once.

"Hey, you're right!" he exclaims. *"There he is again!"*

"Come on," says Jake. "Let's go talk to him."

"Why?" asks Lexi.

"I think he's spying on us," says Jake, arching his eyebrows.

"What?" says Lucas. "How could that be?"

"Yeah," chimes in Lexi. *"We're* the spies, not him!"

"Yes, I know," says Jake. "And so I think we should go talk to him."

Cyril chortles. "Ha! You mean, like, *lean* on him a bit?" he says. "Rough him up? Let him know who's the boss around here?"

"Or maybe just talk to him," says Jake, grinning.

"That's chill," says Cyril, nodding.

"Let's go," says Jake.

Jake starts strolling casually along the street toward the hooded kid; the others follow suit. The kid has his back to Team Spy Gear, but now he looks more alert. Jake glances over at his brother Lucas, who suddenly looks very nervous.

"What's crackin', bro?" asks Jake.

Lucas points across the park.

"Check it out," he says.

On the far side of the park, maybe a hundred yards away, a pack of boys is emerging from a drainage ditch. Even from this distance, you can hear the snarling and spitting and cursing.

"The Wolf Pack!" cries Cyril. "Gads!"

A large, dark-haired boy lopes ahead of the pack. His knuckles scrape the ground, and he drags a deer carcass with his teeth. Okay, maybe not. But he's a big bad kid. Plus he's unfriendly.

"Brill!" gasps Lucas.

Brill Joseph is the alpha thug of this local gang of bullies that call themselves the Wolf Pack. He's fourteen, Jake and Cyril's age. His second in command, Wilson

Wills, is also fourteen. The rest of the pack is a mixed-age group, with the older boys keeping the younger ones in line via fear, intimidation, daily beatings, and large bags of candy, especially lollipops.

Team Spy Gear ducks behind a nearby park equipment shed.

"I don't think they saw us," says Cyril with relief. "Either that, or they just ate their fill of flesh elsewhere and thus aren't hungry at this moment."

Lexi peeks around the shed. "What the donkey are they doing?" she asks.

The boys peek too.

The pack has assembled in the playground area and seems to be . . . what, training? Brill and Wilson bark at boys as they scale ladders, dive down tube slides, crawl over climbing structures, and scramble through the brutal kiddie obstacle courses. It looks like a Marine Corps boot camp. In particular, they go across the pulley ride over and over: a handle on a pulley-wheel that runs the length of a long track. You grab the handle, take a running leap off a low platform, and then ride down the track while hanging from the handle.

"Very strange," says Jake.

"I don't like the looks of it," says Lucas.

"Do you suppose that pulley ride has some significance?" asks Cyril. "Or did someone just throw it in the book to fill up space?"

Jake glances at me. "Hard to say," he says.

Now he turns back up the street. The strange kid still loiters near the bus stop. His hooded head jerks toward the Wolf Pack in the distance, but other than that he seems very relaxed.

Lucas nods toward the kid and says, "What if he's, like, a pack sentry?"

Cyril gasps. "Holy cod socks," he says. "You could be right."

"Maybe he *wants* us to approach him," says Lucas. "Maybe it's a trap."

Suddenly a car horn blares behind them. The four kids spin around to see a driver waving from a blue Toyota Avalon. They all wave back. But it quickly becomes clear that the man is not waving at them. He's waving at someone up the street.

Then the driver stops waving and frowns.

The team turns back toward the kid—or, as we shall henceforth call him, The Kid.

"Hey, where'd he go?" asks Lexi.

Cyril stares up the street. "Whoa," he says. "He vamoosed!"

The team stares at the spot, now vacated, where The Kid had been standing. Look, Willow Park is a *big* park. Except for a few small trees, the area is flat, grassy, and very open for several hundred feet. Beyond the park, just across Willow Road, sits Carlos Santana Middle School, a great hibernating sphinx that hungrily pulps children into Kid Juice and drinks it when it's awake.

Frowning, Jake says, "That's insane. He was just *there*." He scans the landscape.

"Maybe he ran behind the school," says Lexi, eyes flashing.

"So quickly?" says Lucas. "He can't be that fast."

Lexi looks excited. "Maybe he climbed a tree!" she exclaims. Lexi loves trees.

But Jake abruptly turns and jogs back toward the blue Avalon on the street. He leans down at its open window.

"Hey there, Mr. Latimer," he says.

"Hello, Jake Bixby," says the man in the car, who may or may not be named Latimer. Okay, okay—it *is* Mr. Latimer. He's been in enough Spy Gear books that you know Mr. Latimer when you see him.

"Were you waving at us?" asks Jake quickly.

"No," says Mr. Latimer. "I didn't see you until just now." Now Cyril, Lucas, and Lexi arrive next to Jake.

"Howdy, kids," says Mr. Latimer.

"Howdy, Mr. Latimer," says Cyril. He reaches in and shakes the man's hand.

"How's the family, Cyril?" asks Mr. Latimer.

"Excellent," barks Cyril. "No recent embarrassing incidents. We had a pretty big argument about rice the other day, but fortunately it didn't escalate further than the stuff I lobbed at my sister."

"Aren't you an only child?" asks Mr. Latimer.

"I am now," says Cyril.

Mr. Latimer smiles and nods.

"So . . . who were you waving at?" asks Jake.

"A kid up there by the bus stop," says Mr. Latimer, pointing. "But then he skated off across the school grounds." Mr. Latimer pauses, looking confused. "Very fast," he adds.

"Skated?" repeats Jake.

"Yes, skated," says Mr. Latimer.

"On the grass?" asks Cyril.

"Yes, on the grass," says Mr. Latimer.

"Do you know him?" asks Jake.

"Not really," says Mr. Latimer. "He's new in town. I talked to him yesterday." He pauses again, then adds: "Sort of."

Lexi steps to the window. "What do you mean, Mr. Latimer?" she asks.

Cyril looks at her. "Clearly he means 'sort of,'" he says. "Are you deaf?"

"What?" she says, then starts hooting with laughter. "I can't hear you!"

Cyril rolls his eyes. "Middle schoolers are so immature," he says.

"She *ruined* you," howls Lucas.

"No, she didn't."

"Yes!" chortles Lucas.

"No way!" says Cyril.

"Yes way."

"She didn't."

"Did."

"Didn't."

"Ruined!"

"Not!"

"Guys," says Jake calmly. "Please." He turns to Mr. Latimer. "Mr. Latimer, you say you 'sort of' talked to The Kid. What exactly do you mean?"

Mr. Latimer opens a bottle of Gatorade and takes a good swig. He's been living out of his car for almost four years now, looking for an on-ramp to the Expressway that runs through Carrolton. People in town don't want him to leave, though. So they keep giving him bad directions, and he ends up back in the neighborhood. Here, he keeps a good eye on things. People like that.

"Well, Jake, I was in the parking lot of the Country Market doing my taxes," he said. "And the boy walked past my car."

"Wait," says Cyril. "Did you say *taxes?*"

"Yes, Cyril," says Mr. Latimer.

"But you're homeless," says Cyril.

"Yes, but like most people, I want the government to know everything about my life and finances," says Mr. Latimer. "That way they can keep better track of me, which makes me safer."

"Gotcha," says Cyril with a wink and a nod.

"So The Kid walked past your car?" repeats Jake.

"Yes," says Mr. Latimer.

"And what happened?" asks Jake.

"I called *hello* out the window," says Mr. Latimer.

"And his response?" asks Jake.

"Not a word," says Mr. Latimer.

Jake looks frustrated, so Cyril steps forward. He says, "If I may redirect the witness, your honor." He turns to Mr. Latimer. "Mister Latimer. On the day in question, did this so-called 'The Kid' give you any indication he'd been spoken to?"

"Why, yes," replies Mr. Latimer. "Yes, he did."

"Can you elaborate for us?" asks Cyril.

Mr. Latimer opens his glove compartment and pulls out a red sheet of paper. It's a "Lost Dog" flyer. Mr. Latimer hands it out the window to Cyril.

"He gave me this," says Mr. Latimer. "Then he just walked on."

Team Spy Gear gathers around to take a look at the flyer.

Under the words "Lost Dog" is a picture of a Slorg.

3

OLD ACQUAINTANCES

Yes, the Slorg! And let me say it again, but louder: *the Slorg!* Cyril points at the flyer.

"Lost *dog*?" he reads. "That's hilarious!" He starts laughing loudly.

"Hey!" says Lexi happily. "Look who it is!"

The Slorg is an old acquaintance of Team Spy Gear, as is Mr. Latimer, of course. (Can you spot more old acquaintances in this chapter?) As you can see by Lexi's reaction, the mighty Slorg isn't quite as scary as back when Spy Gear fans first met him in Book 2 of the Spy Gear Adventures series, entitled *The Massively Multiplayer Mystery*. Back then, Team Spy Gear knew only that the fierce-looking Slorg was a genetically engineered beast created by Viper.

Jake and Lucas exchange a look.

"This is very odd," says Jake.

"Yes," says Mr. Latimer, studying the flyer. "That's clearly not a normal dog."

"It's a Slorg," says Lexi.

"Dude!" says Cyril to Lexi, slapping his forehead. He leans close to her and quietly murmurs, "Ix-nay on the Org-slay."

"Why?" she asks innocently.

"Because it's a secret!" yells Cyril.

Lexi gives Mr. Latimer a sideways glance. She says, "Oh."

Lucas steps up to defend his best friend.

"Cyril," he says. "I think Mr. Latimer knows what's going on around here."

"Yes, I've seen this dog many times," says Mr. Latimer, nodding. "It was hanging around Stoneship Woods last fall. Then it disappeared."

"See?" says Lucas to Cyril.

"And now it's back," says Mr. Latimer.

What? Everyone stares at him, including the Pope and those two guys in Iowa who are reading this book way too closely.

"It's . . . back?" asks Jake.

"Yes, Jake," says Mr. Latimer.

"You've seen the Slorg again?"

"Yes," says Mr. Latimer. "That's why I was waving to the boy. I wanted to tell him I've seen his dog."

Lexi is excited. "When did you see it?" she asks. "Where?"

"Two nights ago," says Mr. Latimer. "It was sniffing along the edge of Stoneship Woods again." He squints as he remembers. "It was pretty dark; I only saw its outline, and the red glowing eyes. It kept rising up on its hind legs, looking up into tree branches." He frowns. "What a strange breed of dog!"

Lucas frowns. "You saw the, uh . . . *dog* moving around Stoneship Woods?" he asks.

"That's right," replies Mr. Latimer.

"Did you hear any alarms go off?" asks Lucas.

"Gee," says Mr. Latimer. "No, I didn't. That's odd, isn't it?"

Jake catches a glimpse of movement near the middle school. Frowning, he turns in that direction. Then he stiffens.

"Guys," he says quietly.

The way he says it gets everyone's attention, even Mr. Latimer's. They follow his gaze.

Up the street in the Santana school parking circle, a small, jittery dust devil swirls and shudders side to side. At one point it collapses to the ground, but then rises up into a distinct whirlwind again. It's only two or three feet high.

This is odd because the day is quite calm. No wind whatsoever.

"Oh, no," groans Cyril.

"Yes," nods Jake. "Maybe The Kid isn't a kid at all."

"He's a flipping *nanoswarm!*" exclaims Lucas.

"No wonder he's looking for the Slorg!" says Lexi angrily. "He seeks revenge!"

Okay. If you're new to Spy Gear Adventures, you have no clue what anybody is talking about right now. And guess what? *Too bad for you!* That's what you get for starting a six-book series by reading Book 6 first. Now, you loyal readers who've been following Team Spy Gear from the very beginning certainly remember the nasty nanoswarms of Book 4: *The Doomsday Dust*. You might also recall that the Slorg, a powerful pantherlike beast, reappeared in that adventure and actually defended Jake, Lucas, and Lexi from the attack of a gigantic nanoswarm. And finally, you no doubt remember that when government agents rescued the Slorg in Book 4, they took the creature into captivity to study it. There, Agency scientists learned that Viper's fearsome black beast was in fact . . . a berry-eating vegetarian.

Whoa. Sounds like a pretty good book. I might have to read it.

"Let's *get* that kid," says Lexi darkly.

"But how?" asks Lucas. "How can we 'collect' him? We don't have a vacuum cleaner handy."

Mr. Latimer leans out his car window. "What the dickens are you children talking about?"

Lucas points at the swirling entity.

"That *thing* there is no dust devil," he says. "It's an intelligent, deadly swarm of microscopic nanoparticles."

Mr. Latimer squints, thinking. After a few seconds, he says, "Hmmmm."

"My sentiments exactly," says Cyril.

Jake is already running toward the swarm. The others follow, and Mr. Latimer trolls his car up the street alongside them. But halfway there, Jake halts.

"Check it out," he says.

Up ahead, a black-hooded figure peeks around the far side of the Santana school building, just behind the nanoswarm.

Lexi spots him too. "It's The Kid!" she whispers.

Yes, yes it is. Now The Kid creeps around the building toward the little whirlwind.

"So The Kid is *not* the swarm," says Cyril. He rubs his chin. "The Kid is The Kid. And the swarm is the swarm. Thus it appears that each thing is *itself*, rather than something *other* than itself." He nods sagely. "What a clever ruse."

"Look, he's trying to nab the swarm too!" whispers Lexi.

"This is utterly *whack*," says Lucas. "What should we do?"

Jake turns calmly and says, "Let's just watch."

The team watches as The Kid tiptoes toward the

whirlwind. He steps lightly into the school parking lot. Suddenly, the nanoswarm flashes red and pulses up and down rapidly. The Kid makes a stunning pounce; he moves like a jungle cat! But the swarm scatters. It looks like a small fireworks explosion, spinning outward in ribbons of red. *Wow!*

"Holy haddock!" cries Lucas.

"What's he doing now?" asks Lexi.

The Kid raises both hands, palms forward. Red spirals of the nanodust freeze in place. They start wriggling in the air like tortured swirls of living confetti. *Wow!*

Lexi abruptly bursts into a sprint. "Hey, kid!" she yells. *"Hey!"*

The Kid's black hood jerks in Team Spy Gear's direction.

"Lexi!" hisses Lucas after her. "What are you doing?"

But she keeps running.

The others follow her.

The Kid quickly lowers his hands and ducks back behind the school building. The red nanoribbons flash white and silver, and then start wriggling wildly. Within seconds they completely dissolve.

Lexi continues her dash toward the school. Jake has to sprint hard to pull even with her. As he does, he catches the determined look in her eye.

"Dude!" he gasps, running beside her.

"Gotta catch him!" she huffs.

31

"Why?"

"See his face."

When they turn the first corner, they find nothing; The Kid has already rounded the next corner of the building. Jake lengthens his stride and then skids on gravel into the playground at the rear of the school. He catches a brief glimpse of The Kid, who is already clear across the road that runs behind school, Ridgeview Drive. He's plunging into the dark trees of Stoneship Woods.

Jake stops in his tracks.

"He went into Stoneship," he says to the others as they catch up.

"Stoneship!" exclaims Lucas. "He can't go in there!"

"But he did," says Jake.

"Great," says Cyril, looking ill.

Jake glances at his bud. "What's wrong, dog?"

"You know, I've really enjoyed this summer vacation," says Cyril bleakly.

Jake just gazes at him, waiting.

"Do you want to know why?" says Cyril.

"No."

"Okay, I'll *tell* you why," says Cyril. "Ever since Stoneship became off-limits, I've been sleeping like a *baby*, Jake. I don't have those dreams where angry trees surround my house and throw diseased ferrets through the windows." Cyril sighs. "Anyway, I suppose this makes it final. We'll be going back into the woods soon."

"Yes," says Jake.

Cyril gives a resigned nod. "Can I finish writing my novel first?" he asks.

"No time for that," says Jake, grinning.

"My last will and testament?"

"Nope."

Cyril looks at the woods. "Okay," he says. "But I'm not going in without a broadaxe."

"Well, squad," says Lucas. "We've certainly got plenty of disturbing new data that needs digesting." He rubs his hands together in excitement. "Time for a strategic planning session!" Other than gadgets and gizmos, of course, strategic planning sessions are Lucas Bixby's favorite things in the world.

A car horn beeps. The kids watch as Mr. Latimer pulls his Toyota next to them. A red light on Ridgeview Drive delayed him a bit, plus he had to drive all the way around the school grounds.

Mr. Latimer calls out of his window: "Did you find him?"

"No," says Jake. "He ran into the woods."

"Oh, no," says Mr. Latimer. "I hope he doesn't get any West Nile mosquito bites."

"West Nile?" says Cyril, eyeing the dark trees. "If that's *all* that happens to him in there, the dude should throw a party."

One of the large cottonwoods scowls and makes an obscene gesture.

"I *saw* that!" shouts Cyril, pointing at it.

An hour later the team sits in the Bixby backyard.

The sun is high and hot, but Mr. Bixby has built a small redwood gazebo near the back fence, so the kids lounge lazily on lawn chairs in the shade of its canopy roof.

"It's hot," says Cyril.

"Hot," agrees Jake.

"Hot hot," says Cyril.

"Hot hot hot hot," says Jake. "Hot."

Lexi looks at a small tree nearby.

"Maybe it's cooler up higher," she yawns.

"Why?" says Cyril.

Good question. No tree in the Bixby's housing development is more than ten feet tall because everything's so new. The houses along Agincourt Drive all look alike—same shape, same color, same pets, plus almost everybody named their son Justin, so there're an awful lot of Justins. As a result, people are constantly going "home" to the wrong house. Men walk in a front door, shout "Honey! I'm home!" and then duck as the actual inhabitants open fire. Oddly enough, sometimes people walk into the wrong house yet find some of their own family members living there. People start redecorating

34

one another's houses. It can get very confusing.

House builders claim they do this on purpose, of course. The idea, they say, is to trick neighbors into meeting each other a lot. This builds a sense of community. It has absolutely nothing to do with the fact that it's much cheaper to order four bajillion of the same construction materials and then make the same house over and over and over again.

Lucas is asleep in his chair and mumbling.

"Okay, let's review what we know," he mumbles, twitching a few times. He moans loudly, and then hisses, *"Let's get organized!"*

Lexi reaches over and shakes Lucas. He awakens with a snort.

"Wake up," says Lexi.

Blinking, Lucas looks around.

He says, "Wow! What a dream!" Then he grabs his Spy Gear Casebook and a pencil. "Okay, so let's review what we know. *Let's get organized!*"

"Yes, by golly!" says Cyril, slamming his right fist into his left palm. Then, amazingly, he slams his right fist into his *right* palm too. Go ahead, try it yourself. We'll just wait here for the next 150 years until you do it.

"So what's first?" asks Lucas, pencil poised.

"First," says Jake, "we have reason to believe that the Slorg and at least one swarm of nanites are loose somewhere in the Stoneship Woods vicinity."

Lucas writes rapidly. "Okay," he says. "What else?"

"Second," says Lexi, "there's The Kid."

Lucas nods. "And what do we know about this Kid?" he asks.

Lexi thinks hard. "Ummm," she says. "Well. Uh. He wears a hood."

Lucas nods, writing. "He wears a black hoodie, even on the hottest day of summer," he says. "That's certainly worth noting. What else?"

"He skates?" replies Lexi.

Lucas writes, nodding. "According to an eyewitness report from Mr. Latimer," he says, "this Kid can skate really fast across unusual surfaces, like grass. What else?"

Cyril stands up from his lawn chair.

"He's ugly," he says. Then he holds out his arms and bows.

"We don't know that!" says Lucas. "We've never seen his face!"

Cyril points at him. "*Exactly* my point!" he says. He sits with a smug smile.

"And one other thing," says Jake. "He's handing out Missing Slorg flyers and chasing nanites." Jake folds his arms, thinking about this. "Which is about the goofiest thing ever, except for the way he froze that little swarm when it tried to disperse. Let's face it, team—*that* was beastly."

Everyone nods at that. Lucas continues taking notes.

"The Lost Slorg flyer is my favorite thing of all time,"

says Cyril. "The insanity of that is insane beyond all madness." He chuckles. "It's so crazy it kind of makes me admire the guy."

"Why would some kid be looking for the Slorg?" asks Lucas. "How does he even know the Slorg exists?"

"Maybe he fed it some berries once and they became friends," says Lexi.

Lucas smiles. "Sounds like something *you'd* do," he says to her.

"You bet I would!" says Lexi.

They pound fists.

"And why was The Kid trying to catch the nanoswarm?" asks Jake. "Ideas?"

He looks around. Everybody just shrugs.

"Maybe he was looking for evidence," says a deep voice nearby.

The four kids turn to the voice. A very hugely large man of extreme massiveness stands at the back fence. He wears a well-stuffed camping backpack. His dreadlocks look like a nest of black snakes.

"Evidence?" says Lucas, grinning at the big guy. "Are you saying The Kid's, like, a *cop*?"

Everybody laughs at this . . . except the big guy.

Before we end this chapter, let's take a quick peek over at Central Asia, shall we?

It's really a lovely region.

The central highlands are stark and beautiful. Its two great rivers, the Amu Darya and the Syr Darya, carve spectacular valleys through the mountains. The northern steppes are wild and dry and empty. Many strange things happen here.

Check out the action on that high mountain pass, for example.

Three goggled men climb with great difficulty up a red rock canyon. After what seems an eternity, they reach a granite ledge overlooking a massive cave mouth. Its opening tilts upward; its floor drops at a shallow angle into the ground. Exhausted, the men lean against large boulders. All three are dressed in mountain camouflage.

The man in the lead turns to his companions, who drink from flasks.

"How are you doing, Gibbs?" he asks.

"Better, sir," says Gibbs. His voice sounds raspy and strained.

"Are you sure?" asks the leader.

"Yes," says Gibbs. "I . . . I don't know what got into me, sir."

The leader turns to the other man. "What about you, Mason?" he asks.

"I'm good," says Mason.

"Anything from Omega?" asks the leader.

Mason rips open a Velcro side pocket on his wind jacket and pulls out a slick black PDA. He punches a button and its screen lights up.

"Nothing, sir," he says.

Now all three gaze down a rocky slope at the jagged cave opening. It is roughly twenty feet wide and ten feet high—easily large enough to drive a truck into. It is also very, very dark.

In fact, the cave's darkness looks almost . . . unnatural.

The squad leader pushes his goggles up onto his forehead.

"Let's get set up," he says to the others.

Mason slides off his backpack, opens it, and pulls out a gray metal tripod. He hands it over to Gibbs, who sets it upright. Then Mason pulls out an odd-looking device—a long tube that looks like a cross between a gun and a camera. It's clearly quite heavy. He attaches it to the top of the tripod.

The squad leader slips a small spy scope out of his sleeve pouch and trains it on the cave.

Gibbs tries to steady the tripod. Suddenly, a loud piercing shriek rises from the cave mouth. The shriek is so deep and powerful and harsh, it's as if the cave itself were screaming in pain. Gibbs staggers backward, clapping his hands over his ears. Both the leader and Mason turn to him in alarm.

"Agent Gibbs?" calls the leader. "Gibbs!"

Gibbs turns a savage gaze on his companions. He starts hissing like a rabid cat.

His eyes are completely black, as if coated with oil.

ODD HOUSE

Lexi leaps to her feet and runs to the big hairy man at the Bixbys' back fence. "Yo, cousin!" she cries, holding up her hand for a high five.

The man just stares down at the tiny girl's raised hand.

"Look," he says. "Just because we're related doesn't mean I have to act like an idiot around you."

Lexi snickers. Marco always cracks her up. But she keeps up her hand, waiting for the high five. After a few seconds, Marco shakes his head, reaches down, and taps her hand.

"How was Uzbekistan?" asks Jake.

"It was good, Bixby," says Marco. "I liked everything except the food, the people, the accommodations, and the geography."

Cyril guffaws. "So everything else was *fabulous*, then?"

Marco slings his backpack over the fence and sets it down in the Bixby backyard. Then he hops over, landing heavily in the grass. The fence runs along a drainage culvert behind the Bixby property. Beyond the culvert is city-protected open space, a natural prairie habitat with trails for hiking.

"So what do you mean, The Kid was 'looking for evidence'?" asks Lucas.

"Ah, little Bixby gets right back to the point," says Marco. "Don't you want to hear more about Uzbekistan first? Dude, I've been gone for, like, six weeks. Maybe I learned something."

"Hey, Marco," says Jake.

"What?" answers Marco.

"Tell us about Uzbekistan."

"I can't," says Marco. "Top secret."

Jake grins. "Of course," he says.

"Wait!" says Lexi. "Did you hear that the Slorg is back?"

Marco nods. "Yes," he says.

"Did it escape or something?"

Marco nods, looking darkly amused. He says, "Our competent friends at the Agency left not one but *two* security doors open for six hours last week."

Kids, let me take a minute here to clarify a few things for you.

Spy Gear fans, all forty-eight billion of you, know

that this big man is Marco. Marco has a long history with Team Spy Gear; in fact, he was the team's very first nemesis back in Book 1: *The Secret of Stoneship Woods*. He's a world-class computer hacker, and now he's arguably the team's most important ally. We also learned recently that Marco happens to be Lexi Lopez's cousin (once removed on his mother's side).

"Dude, you're, like, buff," says Jake to Marco.

Marco looks sullen. "I've been rock climbing," he says. He steps up onto the gazebo.

"You don't look too happy about it," says Jake.

"I don't like exerting myself," says Marco.

"So why did you?"

"They made me," says Marco.

Jake's eyebrows lift. "The Agency?"

"Yes." Marco folds his massive arms across his chest. "I went places in Uzbekistan where no sane man should go."

Cyril jumps up. "You were huge before, but now look at you," he says. "You're a beast." He claps Marco on the shoulder. "In fact, I'd have to say you've achieved maximum beastability."

"Don't touch me," says Marco.

"Sorry," says Cyril.

"So tell us some nonsecret stuff about Uzbekistan," says Jake.

"The mountains are grim and full of unpleasant

surprises," says Marco. "I spent five days in one of the most godforsaken outposts you could possibly imagine."

"Doing what?" asks Jake.

"Looking for Omega," he says.

"Omega?"

Marco nods. "The inside man," he says.

Now Lucas explodes to his feet. "Wait!" he shouts. "You mean . . . the source of the Omega Link messages? *Is that what you mean?*"

Marco winces. "Could you shriek just a little bit *quieter*, Bixby?" he asks.

"Sorry," says Lucas, bouncing on his toes. "Wow! So he's, like, code-named Omega and he's in Uzbekistan. Why? What's he doing in Uzbekistan?"

"Scratching at his sandfly bites," says Marco unhappily.

Jake laughs. "By 'inside man,' do you mean he's inside Viper's organization?" he asks.

Marco says, "Correct."

"So, what exactly was your role?" asks Lucas.

Marco gives him a look. "I'm only good at one thing," he says.

Lucas nods. "Hacking site codes," he says.

Cyril points at Marco's hair. "Plus it's always good to have a yeti on the team," he says.

Marco gives Cyril a hostile grin.

Cyril gulps. "Don't crush me," he says.

Now Marco turns to Lexi. He crouches down to her

eye level and pulls an envelope from his back pocket. Then he jams it at her.

Lexi takes it. "What's this?" she asks.

"It's a note to your mother," he replies.

"From who?"

"From me."

Lexi frowns. "I don't get it."

Marco sighs. "Our mothers were great friends when they were little," he says. "I heard stories." He nods at the letter and stands up tall again. "I just wanted to tell her hello."

Lexi cradles the envelope like it's precious and breakable.

"Okay," she says.

Suddenly the Bixbys' back door bursts open and a small woman steps onto the porch.

"Excuse me?" she calls out. She starts descending the porch steps.

"Uh-oh," says Lucas.

"Speaking of mothers," murmurs Jake, eyes wide.

"Excuse me?" calls Mrs. Bixby aggressively as she crosses the yard. "Do I know you, young man?"

Marco is more than twice the size of Mrs. Bixby. But frankly, if both of them were thrown into a jungle pit and only one could emerge alive, I'd bet the entire International Space Station on Mrs. Bixby.

"It's cool, Mom," calls Jake. "This is Lexi's cousin Marco."

"Oh!" says Mrs. Bixby. "Well, then! Nice to meet you, Marco." She steps up onto the gazebo and extends her little hand to Marco.

Marco wraps his bear paw around her bird claw and gives it a quick shake.

"Right," he says.

"Can I get you some lemonade?" asks Mrs. Bixby. "Iced tea, perhaps? Where do you work? Do I know your parents? What level of classes did you take in school?" She smiles sweetly. "I'd love to hear about your SAT scores."

Marco manages a tight smile. He turns to Jake.

"Help me," he says.

"Just do your best," says Jake, grinning.

Lucas leans closer. "That's all we ask, is just your best effort, Marco."

Marco turns back to Mrs. Bixby.

"I have to go," he says.

"Why?" asks Mrs. Bixby.

Marco is stunned by this question. For a second, he just stares down at her. Then he squats to open his backpack. He pulls out a manila envelope and hands it to Jake.

"Photos from Uzbekistan," he says. "You'll find them interesting."

"Sweet," says Jake.

Marco points at him and says, "Let's talk later, Bixby." With a significant look, he adds, "I have more news."

Jake raises his eyebrows. "Okay," he says.

Marco turns back to Mrs. Bixby. He opens his mouth to speak, but then just shakes his head. He slings his huge backpack onto a shoulder and tromps around the house to the street.

"Nice meeting you!" calls Mrs. Bixby after him.

Cyril gives a Roman salute. "Good-bye, large man," he calls.

Mrs. Bixby turns to the children.

"His backpack looked *extremely* well-organized," she says, smiling brightly.

Two hours later, Jake Bixby walks alone down Ridgeview Drive.

Marco's manila envelope of photos is tucked under Jake's arm and he holds his cell phone to his ear. After viewing Marco's Uzbekistan pictures, the team decided to split up for separate tasks.

Jake's job: Make copies of the photos and contact Marco. He has all but two of the original photos in the envelope; those two he left at home with Lucas for some Internet research.

Jake listens to his phone for a few seconds, then speaks: "Uh, Marco, hey dude, this is Jake Bixby, leaving a message . . . well, of *course* I'm leaving a message, this is your voice message center, right? Heh. Well." Jake winces. "Anyway, I'm heading downtown. Let's meet at the ice cream shop for a chat about your Uzbekistan photos. We found them kind of confusing. So if you could just, you know . . . give me a call back when you get this message, that would be, uh, that, that would . . . *yikes!*"

Jake quickly flips the phone shut and slips it in his pocket as he stops in his tracks.

Up the street, a girl with purple hair, purple-tinted glasses, purple lipstick, and a long purple skirt is walking toward him. She reads a slim book as she walks. Jake is frozen with indecision.

The girl looks up and sees him.

Her step stutters and her eyes widen for a second—an involuntary sign of recognition. But she quickly recovers her lethal cool. Her stride slows to a careless strut. Her eyebrows remain slightly arched. Yes, guys, you know this look: that skull-piercing, world-weary, "disgusted-with-the-immaturity-of-boys" look that girls are so *freakishly* good at.

As she approaches, she says, "Bixby."

Jake stands there, smiling like an idiot. "Barbie," he says.

She passes him, then stops, looking back. "Do you always stand in one spot for, like, long periods of time?" she asks.

Jake gazes down at his feet. "Yes," he says.

Barbie nods, looking at him.

"Actually, I *was* walking, like, before," says Jake, gesturing back behind him. "But then I saw you and stopped, and, uh, then I was going to . . . start again. You know, start walking." He grimaces. "Yeah."

"Interesting story," says Barbie.

"So what are you reading?" asks Jake, nodding at her book.

"Poetry," she says.

"Why?" asks Jake. "It's summer."

"So?"

"So are you getting a head start on high school assignments or something?" asks Jake. "I mean . . . is this something I should be doing too? Because if there's some pursuit-of-excellence-type thing that I'm not doing, my mom will be very depressed."

"No," says Barbie. A very small smile creeps across her lips like a thin purple worm.[5,6] "I'm reading because I like to read."

Jake nods. "That's tight," he states.

This girl, of course, is Barbie Bickle. Her own poetry and her keen observations helped Team Spy Gear in the last book, *The Shrieking Shadow*. Barbie is different from most other Carrolton kids, and so naturally they have to

5. Kids, that's a "simile." Look for more school-type stuff this chapter. For example, I plan to factor a complex polynomial somewhere within the next three pages. Keep your eyes peeled!

6. Please do not literally "peel your eyes." This is a "metaphor." It means keep your eyes open and pay close attention. Actually peeling your eyes would be unbelievably painful.

make fun of her. They call her "Psycho Chick."

But Jake Bixby doesn't.

Barbie starts to speak, then stops. She seems to debate within her head whether or not to go on. Then she speaks anyway.

"So, uh, where were you going?" she asks cautiously. "You know . . . before you . . . stopped walking."

"Oh, I was headed downtown," says Jake.

Barbie nods. There is an uncomfortable pause. Did you know that plants breathe in carbon dioxide and breathe out oxygen? The next day, Jake scratches his cheek. He shuffles the manila envelope from hand to hand.

"What's in the envelope?" asks Barbie. She rolls her eyes as if disgusted at herself for asking such an insipid question.

Jake holds up the envelope and looks at it. He thinks for a few hours, then opens it. He pulls out a pack of glossy eight-by-ten photographs.

He holds up the top photo and turns it toward Barbie Bickle.

"What does this look like to you?" he asks.

Barbie takes a step closer. She wears a perfume that smells like jasmine incense. Jake's head explodes, but he manages to inhale hard enough to suck his brains back into his skull before Barbie notices.

"Hmmm," she murmurs. She leans closer. "I'd say that's a close-up shot of the Happy Grotto."

Jake is stunned. He flips the photo around and studies it.

"Holy zeppelin, you're right!" he exclaims. "That's *exactly* what it is. No wonder it looked so familiar." He shakes his head. "That's very bizarre."

The Happy Grotto is a rock-sculpture playground in the Soccer Complex, next to the parking lot. Little kids clamber all over a Stonehenge-like garden of rocks built in a sandpit. Jake knows it well; he grew up playing in it. He's embarrassed he didn't recognize it.

Barbie gives him a quizzical look. "Why is a photo of the Happy Grotto so bizarre?" she asks.

"Because it was taken in Uzbekistan," says Jake.

"Uzbekistan?" repeats Barbie, looking skeptical.

"Supposedly," says Jake, nodding.

"Hmmm," says Barbie again. "Can I see the others?"

Jake hesitates. Some of the photos in the packet are kind of odd and disturbing.

Barbie is quick to note his pause. "Never mind," she says.

"Actually, I'd like to show them to you," says Jake with all honesty. "But . . ."

"It's cool," says Barbie. Suddenly her eyes dart up over Jake's shoulder. She squints and adds, "There he is again."

Jake turns and, sure enough, there he is again: The Kid! He walks up Ridgeview Drive, heading away from them. Within seconds he disappears around a curve in the road.

"You've seen that Kid too?" asks Jake.

"Oh, yeah," says Barbie. "Ever since he moved in, I see him everywhere."

Jake turns to Barbie. "When was this?"

"You mean, when did he move in?" asks Barbie. "About three weeks ago."

"Do you know where he lives?" asks Jake with a hint of excitement.

"Yeah," says Barbie.

Jakes eyes widen. "Where?"

"Follow me," says Barbie.

As she starts walking up Ridgeview Drive, Jake falls in behind her. She stops and looks back at him.

"Actually, Bixby, I'd prefer that you walk *beside* me," she says dryly. "'Follow me' is, like, a figure of speech."

"Right," says Jake.

They walk together up the street. After rounding the curve in Ridgeview Drive, Barbie stops and points to a house.

"That's it," she says.

"That?"

"That."

Of course, it looks like every other house on the street. Just another gray-and-white suburban home, like a few hundred others on Carrolton's winding streets. Jake studies the house carefully, but finds nothing out of the ordinary.

"You're *sure* this is where he lives?" asks Jake.

"Absolutely," says Barbie. "I live right there."

She points to the house next door.

"You live next door to The Kid?" asks Jake.

Barbie nods. "Why are you so interested in him?" she asks.

Jake stares at the house. "Have you noticed anything *strange* about him?"

"I've never seen his face, which is kind of odd, I guess," says Barbie. "He's always got that hood up." She looks at the house and thinks a second. "And then there's all the weird stuff in his backyard at night."

"What kind of stuff?" asks Jake.

Barbie says, "Before his family moved in, they had a super-high security fence built around the back. It's, like, three feet higher than everybody else's security fence. After that I heard construction sounds for a week or so, plus lots of running water."

"Running water?"

Barbie shrugs. "I figured they were building a swimming pool."

"That makes sense," says Jake.

"But at night, when I sit on my deck and read, I hear splashing and, like . . . *snorting* over there," says Barbie.

"In his backyard?" asks Jake.

Barbie nods and says, "And weird machine sounds."

"What kind of machine?"

Barbie looks a little unsettled. "Hard to say," she says. "It doesn't sound like anything I've heard before. I don't know . . . maybe like a large vacuum cleaner or something."

Jake frowns. "Weird," he says.

Barbie nods slowly. "And then there's the colored lights," she says.

Jake freezes. "What?" he asks.

Barbie looks at the house. "The other night I heard the machine sound again. I looked up and saw lights glowing: red, green, blue. They were reflected off the leaves of the tree in his backyard. I heard voices over there too." She shrugs. "I figured maybe it was a dance party, except I didn't hear any music."

"Colored lights," murmurs Jake, gritting his teeth.

"Is something wrong?" asks Barbie.

Jake turns to her and says, "No . . . no. I just . . ." But then he notices a black car pull to the curb just up the street. Its passenger door bursts open and a familiar figure emerges: a tall beanpole of a man with a big white mustache and a wild shock of white hair dropping from beneath a gaucho hat.

"Dr. Tim!" exclaims Jake.

Wow! Jake hasn't seen Dr. Tim since the end of Book 5: *The Shrieking Shadow*, when the crazy environmental

53

scientist got whisked off by the Agency in a black helicopter. Now Dr. Tim stands next to the black car, staring at The Kid's house.

Then the driver's door opens too. A massive fellow with a blond crew cut steps out onto the street next to Dr. Tim.

Barbie turns to follow Jake's stare.

She says, "Isn't that the crazy lawn dude?"

"Yes," says Jake, grinning. "I haven't seen Dr. Tim in weeks."

Barbie nods. "That guy with him is impossibly huge."

Jake has to agree. The blond man is so big, he's almost inhuman. Massive legs jut out of big baggy cargo shorts, and his arms burst from the short sleeves of a colorful Hawaiian shirt. He looks remarkably strong. From this distance he looks forty or so, roughly Dr. Tim's age. But he's in amazing shape.

Dr. Tim speaks in an animated manner. Then he makes a sudden break toward The Kid's house. The big blond man looks startled and hurries after Dr. Tim. The way he walks looks . . . familiar.

Very familiar.

Stunned, Jake watches as the man suddenly trips on the curb, staggers forward a few steps, then crashes face-first into the lawn. He rolls over quickly and tries to bounce back to his feet, but slams into the mailbox by the curb. His weight is so great that the mailbox starts bending over to the ground. The huge blond man hangs on to the sagging post, trying to regain his balance as the box tilts in slow motion toward the ground.

Barbie starts snickering. "Oh my God, that's funny," she says.

But Jake isn't laughing.

5

DOGS, BUGS, AND SQUIDS

Lucas and Lexi are hunched over a flat-panel monitor.
They sit at the computer desk in the Bixby study, a small
room just off the kitchen. Lucas types rapidly, entering a
string of terms into a search engine called GeoHistory
Plus.

He types UZBEKISTAN ANCIENT STONE SCULPTURE and
then hits the Enter key.

"Hand me the dog, please," he says to Lexi.

She grabs a glossy eight-by-ten photo and hands it to
Lucas. It is a shot of a stone figure—a crude carving, but
without a doubt, it is a statue of the Slorg. This is one of
Marco's Uzbekistan photos.

"Bizarre," says Lucas, looking at it.

"Yeah," says Lexi. "Why would there be a Slorg statue
in Uzbekistan?"

"I don't know."

"Do you think there's more than one Slorg?" she asks.

"I doubt it," says Lucas.

"So then somebody in Uzbekistan carved *our* Slorg."

Lucas gives Lexi a look. "*Our* Slorg?" He grins. "Yes, I guess they did."

Images of old stone statues start popping open in onscreen windows across the monitor. None of them is a Slorg.

"Hmmm. Let me see the bug too," says Lucas.

Lexi hands him a photo of another rock carving. This one is of a frightening insect. A triangle-shaped head sits on a slender neck. It has big, bulbous eyes with two slender antennae and a pointed mouth full of nasty-looking chewing parts. Huge barbed forelegs with sharp hooks on the end extend forward beneath the head and then fold downward. This is clearly a praying mantis.

Lexi shivers. "It gives me the creeps," she says.

"Yes," says Lucas. "I don't like the way he's looking at me."

Lexi nods. "He looks hungry."

Lucas scans through the onscreen stone carvings again. Again, no match. He shakes his head.

"This mantis means something," he says, looking at the bug sculpture.

Okay, here we go again. Recap time! You Spy Gear fans know all about the slim, silver com-link device called the Omega Link. This link served clues from a mysterious source to Team Spy Gear in all five of the previous cases in this series. Unfortunately, the Agency took the Omega Link away from Lucas and the others last spring. But just before that, the device delivered one last set of messages to the team.

One of them seemed odd, almost nonsensical.

It said, simply:

FLUSH THE MANTIS.

By the way, the very last Omega message was this:

PLEASE HELP ME,

BIXBYS.

Anyway, the team has pondered and discussed the strange mantis message for many hours this summer, with little to show for their effort. Experts at the Agency have analyzed FLUSH THE MANTIS thoroughly, too.

Nobody has a clue what it means.

But now, Marco's rock-climbing expedition in Uzbekistan has discovered this rock sculpture. So there *is* a mantis connection, apparently. What it is, nobody knows yet.

"Flush the mantis," says Lucas quietly, staring at the photo.

"Down the toilet?" asks Lexi.

Lucas shakes his head. "Doesn't make sense," he says.

Lexi, as you know, is very good at guessing the meaning of coded messages. But this one has her grasping at straws. Lucas opens his Spy Gear Casebook, which sits on the desk. Here's where he keeps detailed notes about each new mystery that Team Spy Gear tackles. He flips to the page where he jotted down the Omega Link's final sequence of messages:

FLUSH THE MANTIS

ANTIGRAV CONTAINME

DISREGARD NONSENSE STRING

PLEASE

HELP ME, BIXBYS

"Man, we've gone over these a *thousand* times," says Lucas. "And from what Marco says, the Agency has some of the top decryption people in the world working on this—looking for patterns, codes, ciphers, algorithms, symmetric keys, you name it. And they find *nothing*. Nothing that works, anyway."

"Maybe it's not code," says Lexi.

Lucas squints at her. "What?"

"Maybe he just wrote out what he meant to say," says Lexi. "Like, in regular words."

Lucas stares down at the messages. "No way," he says. "That *has* to be code. It's too weird to be, like, a real message."

Lexi shrugs. "'Please help me, Bixbys' doesn't sound like a secret message to me," she says.

Lucas hems and haws a bit. "Well, okay, yeah, *that*," he says. "But that's the very last message. The Omega operative was obviously in a hurry at that point. Maybe he was on the verge of getting caught and didn't have time to encrypt the last lines." Lucas taps the casebook page. "I mean, 'antigrav contain me'? What's up with that? That *has* to be code."

"He stopped in the middle of a word," says Lexi, looking at the message.

"What word?"

"Containment," says Lexi.

Lucas stares at the page. "Add *N* and *T* and you have 'antigrav containment,'" he says. "Huh. Maybe." He shakes his head. "But what's with the bug flushing?"

"I just had my school physical," says Lexi.

Lucas half-ignores her as he tries typing in two new search string terms: ANTIGRAVITY CONTAINMENT. "Okay," he says.

Lexi folds her arms. "The doctor said to drink lots of water," she continues.

"Good advice, I'm sure," says Lucas distractedly.

Lexi leans right into her buddy's face. "She told me water helps *flush toxins* out of my system," she says with an edge. She nods. "Lots of water."

Lucas turns to her. "Flush," he says. "Like a radiator flush or something. Flush out the bad stuff."

Lexi leans back and shrugs.

Suddenly, Lucas's cell phone makes a weird chirp. He whips it out and looks at the display window.

"Text message," he says.

"From who?" asks Lexi.

Lucas flips open his phone. His eyebrows knit together. "'One new message from Unknown Caller,'" he reads. "Huh." He presses the Read button and reads the message that appears: BIXBYS. CONTACT HUNTER, PASS CODE TARHEEL. OMEGA.

Lucas and Lexi both pop their eyes wide open. They look at each other.

"Omega?" they say in unison.

"Write it down," says Lexi.

As Lucas jots the message in his open casebook, he asks, "Who's Hunter?"

Lexi shrugs and shakes her head. "Maybe Marco will know," she says.

Lucas saves the text message before he snaps his phone shut. It rings immediately. He looks at the incoming number, brightens, and flips the phone open again.

"Hey, bro," says Lucas into the phone.

"Dog, meet me downtown at the ice cream shop," says Jake over the phone. "And I mean, like, right now."

Lucas hears the urgency in his big brother's voice. He glances at Lexi, and asks, "What's up?"

"Everything!" says Jake. "You won't believe who's with me."

"Who?"

"You'll see when you get here," says Jake.

"We're on the way," says Lucas, bouncing with energy. "Oh, and we just got a text message from somebody named Omega."

There is a pause as Jake repeats this news to somebody on his end. After a few seconds, Jake says, "Roger that, dude. You've made somebody very excited here. Hurry downtown . . . with all possible speed."

"Will do," says Lucas.

"Wait!" says Jake. Now there's another pause as someone with a ridiculously deep voice talks in the background. Then Jake says: "Bro, please relay the Omega message text." He deepens his voice. "Immediately, please."

Lucas grins, then reads the message.

Jake repeats the message on his end. Then he says, "See you in ten. Peace."

"Peace," says Lucas, and hangs up.

Meanwhile, Cyril strolls along County Road 44 where the road runs between Stoneship Woods and the outer wall of Slurry Water Park. He walks with Cat Horton, his really good friend who's a girl, listening to the sickening screams of kids hurtling down the white water tubes inside the park. He holds an apple in one hand and holds, *ahem*, Cat's hand in his other hand.

This means they're holding hands. *Somebody call the cops!*

"Your hand feels like a separate animal," says Cyril, looking down at it.

"Is that right?" replies Cat, amused.

"Yes," says Cyril. "It's like a sea creature. A squid, perhaps."

"Hey, that's really romantic," says Cat.

"It is?" says Cyril, surprised. "Wow, that was easy." He bobs his hair. "Man, I thought it would be hard to say stuff to girls."

Cat rolls her eyes.

"Wait," says Cyril. "Were you being . . . sarcastic?"

Cat is about to answer, but they're approaching one of the Stoneship Woods checkpoints. Two huge men stand by a white car marked with a Health Department logo. Both men wear mirrored aviator sunglasses. Each has a squiggle of white wire running from his collar up to an earbud in his ear.

Cyril waves to them.

"Hi, guys!" he calls loudly. "How's everything at the ol' Health Department?"

One of the men nods slightly. The other one just ignores him.

"Don't let those West Nile mosquitoes bite you!" calls Cyril as he passes them.

Now both men turn their heads toward him.

Cyril backs away from them down the road, grinning and waving.

"Good-bye, Health Department guys!" he calls.

"Okay, Wong," murmurs Cat. "I think they got your point."

"You think so?" asks Cyril.

As they round a slight bend in the road, Cat halts abruptly. She gestures toward something up ahead. Cyril turns to look.

"Crap!" he says.

Brill Joseph and Wilson Wills move along the Slurry Water Park wall. The two bullies study it closely, barking and pointing up at several features. Here the wall runs right along the shoulder of County Road 44. Directly across the road, massive pin oak branches jut out from Stoneship Woods. The limbs arch over the road to within a few feet of the water park wall.

Brill points to the top of the wall, then at the pin oak branches.

"Okay, *that* looks suspicious," says Cat. "Wouldn't you say?"

Cyril swallows hard.

"Perhaps you'd like me to have a word with the chaps?" he says in his deepest voice. "You know, see what the lads are up to?"

"Cyril, don't be a dork," says Cat. "You don't have to act manly." She grins. "Come on, let's spy on them."

Cyril beams at her. "Ah, a *much* better plan," he says.

She tugs him quickly toward the wall. They flatten

against it and slide sideways about thirty feet to a spot where it angles slightly. Just as Cyril leans out to peek around the angle, crowds of kids inside Slurry Water Park start shrieking in sheer terror.

Cyril pulls his head back and stares up.

"Wow," says Cyril quietly. "Must be an insane new water ride."

"They sound pretty scared," whispers Cat.

They listen for a few seconds.

"Seriously," says Cat, "that sounds like utter panic in there."

Cyril nods. "It does sound like people fleeing and, you know, screaming," he says.

Now his cell phone starts vibrating. He whips it open before it can ring, then whispers, "Hello?"

"Dude," replies Jake. "Get downtown to the ice cream shop. Like, now."

"Why?" whispers Cyril.

"Because I've got huge news," replies Jake. He pauses, then adds: "Why are you whispering?"

"Never mind," whispers Cyril. "I'll be there as soon as I can."

"Come now," insists Jake. "Immediately. No delay."

"Okay, okay." Cyril hangs up and looks over at Cat. He says, "Important meeting."

"Go," she says.

"But . . ."

"No buts," says Cat. She peeks around the wall angle at the bullies. "I'll get to the bottom of their nefarious plan. You go."

"Sure you'll be safe?" asks Cyril.

"Wilson is my cousin, remember?" says Cat. "He won't mess with me." She grins. "I know his mom."

Cat and Cyril look at each other for a second.

"Well, see you later," he croaks.

"Yes," says Cat. Her eyes flicker once down to his lips.

Wait! They're not going to *kiss*, are they? Somebody, please, *call the cops!*

But then Cat just whacks Cyril on the arm. He grins and staggers north, the direction they just came from. *Whew!* That was close.

But Cyril takes no more than twenty steps when he hears a wet, slapping sound above him. He glances up just in time to see two huge, black, rubbery tentacles curl over the top of the Slurry Water Park wall. They clamp onto the top of the wall. Then a third tentacle does the same.

"A mutant land-squid!" gasps Cyril, backing away.

Cyril fears squids, yet finds them endlessly fascinating. He writes about squids all the time on his blog, which every good Spy Gear fan has visited at least once at www.cyrilsblog.com.

Cyril freezes as the thick black body to which the tentacles are attached pulls itself over the wall, two more tentacles trail behind and clamp onto the wall too. Then the five appendages slowly lower the bulky body down. It's very big, about the size of a cow[7]. And its blackness is more than black; in the daylight it looks like a living shadow, so dark you feel like you need a flashlight to see it.

Now Cyril recognizes it for what it truly is: a Black Hand creature like the ones we met earlier in Book 5: *The Shrieking Shadow*.

Suddenly the creature's tentacles let go and it hits the ground like a sack of Armenian yak blubber, with a slimy *splat!* Then it starts scrabbling across County Road 44, heading for the woods. Its wiggly appendages pull it forward with remarkable speed for such a disgustingly blubbery beast.

Cyril watches in horrified fascination.

Then he notices something very, very odd.

Just up the road, the two "Health Department" men at the checkpoint casually watch the black monster approach the tree line. As it enters, the beast triggers a motion detector alarm. Its siren blares loudly! One of the men reaches into his automobile and pulls out what looks like a small remote control device.

He points it at the spot where the black squid-monster crawls into Stoneship Woods. Then he pushes a button on the remote.

7. Plus or minus three gophers.

The alarm siren abruptly stops wailing.

Here's the weird part. The guard tosses the controller back onto the front seat of his car. Then both men return to their task of standing like statues by the road, as if nothing at all had happened.

"Yo, guys!" shouts Cyril at them, waving his arms. "Didn't you *see* that thing?"

One of the checkpoint guards glances over at him. Cyril isn't sure, but he thinks the man has the sliver of a smile on his meaty, impassive face.

6

THE FELLOWSHIP OF THE
WHATEVER

A short time later, a group of eight remarkable people gathers around the big circular table in Ye Olde Ice-Cream Shoppe in downtown Carrolton.

Four are smallish.

Two are biggish.

And two are freakishly huge.

Right now, the place is silent except for the lapping of ice cream from sugar cones. Everyone at the table has a cone except for the huge man in black. He can't lap ice cream because of the digital LP voice-filter mask over his face.

"Come on, dude," says Cyril to the Dark Man. "Jake got to hear your real voice. Why can't we?"

"I said no," rumbles the Dark Man.

"It's not fair," says Cyril.

"It's for your protection, Mr. Wong," says the Dark Man, pulling his black hat lower over his black sunglasses. "As I've explained many times."

"Protection?" asks Cyril. "Why? Would I laugh to death if I heard it?"

"Leave him alone, Wong," says Marco, sitting next to the Dark Man. "Brad's had a very bad day."

"My name is not Brad!" thunders the Dark Man.

Cyril takes another lick of his blueberry sherbet and then sticks his tongue out at the Dark Man.

"Okay, check it out," he says. "Is my tongue purple?"

The Dark Man looks at Cyril.

"Is it?" asks Cyril.

The big man's sigh rumbles with bass vibrato.

"I went to Stanford Law School," he says. "I have a doctorate in counterterrorism studies from St. Andrews in Scotland. I was the youngest London station chief in CIA history. I survived horrors in Lebanon, Nicaragua, and places in Central Asia you've never even *heard* of." He looks around the table. "How did I end up with *you* people?"

Cyril nods. "So is my tongue purple?"

"*Yes!*" booms the Dark Man.

"Sweet!" says Cyril.

Lucas points down at his Spy Gear Casebook, which lies open in front of him. "Okay, so we've drawn a *complete* blank on who this 'Hunter' might be." He looks around the table. How about you, Mr. Latimer? You know every-body in Carrolton."

Mr. Latimer looks stunned. He says, "By golly, I do, don't I?" He starts counting on his fingers.

Lucas smiles. "So does the name *Hunter* ring a bell at all?"

"No, not at all," says Mr. Latimer.

Next to him, Dr. Tim pounds his flat hand loudly on the table.

"I don't like hunters," he says angrily.

Everybody looks at him for a second. Then Marco shakes his head and looks at the Dark Man. "If this mes-sage to little Bixby is really from Omega," he begins, "why can't you—?"

The Dark Man interrupts, gripping the edge of the table. "As I've told you, we have *no idea* who this Omega operative is," he says.

Lucas gives him a stunned look. "Wait. Omega isn't with the Agency?" he asks.

"No," says the Dark Man.

Jake leans forward. "But I thought you had someone, a mole, working within Viper's organization," he says.

"We did," says the Dark Man.

"And he doesn't know who this Omega is?" asks Jake.

The Dark Man hesitates. "We extracted our mole some time ago," he says. "Last winter, actually—after it became clear that someone had hacked into our secure

Omega Link frequency. Our man Dr. Hork[8] is lucky he escaped alive. I contacted him just minutes ago, and he's as stumped as we are about the identity of this Omega operative."

"Was it Viper who hacked your code?" asks Lexi.

The Dark Man glances down at her. "That waffle cone is bigger than you are," he says in a gentler tone.

"Are you suggesting I'm small?" says Lexi, jutting her chin a bit.

"Not at all, Miss Lopez," says the Dark Man. "Yes, clearly Viper cracked our link encryption code, most likely via his short-lived access to quantum computing technology.[9,10] But it seems that this mysterious Omega operative somehow acquired access too." He turns to Lucas. "Hence some of the oddly conflicting messages you received via the Omega Link."

It's true. Many of the message sequences that Team Spy Gear received over the Omega Link (going clear back to Book 2: *The Massively Multiplayer Mystery*) seemed almost like two people dueling over the frequency access—one trying to make contact, and the other trying

8. We met Dr. Hork, the Agency mole working inside Viper's organization, back in Book 3: *The Quantum Quandary*. Then we did other stuff.

9. This happened during Book 3: *The Quantum Quandary*, as well. If you go out and buy that book right now, you'll get a free pony.

10. Of course, you have to pay the pony shipping charges. Fortunately, ponies cost only eight thousand dollars for every half-pony you ship. And you get a 10 percent discount if you ship half now, half later!

to halt the contact. A good example is one of the very last Omega Link transmissions: the partial message

ANTIGRAV CONTAINME

cut off in midstream by

DISREGARD NONSENSE STRING.

Lucas gives the Dark Man a dark look. "Yeah, it's too bad you took the Omega Link away from us," he says. "Then our valuable inside operative wouldn't have to send me text messages over a nonsecure international cellular link that almost any idiot could tap."

The Dark Man turns and just looks at Lucas for a few seconds. Then he nods and says, "You make a good point, young Mister Bixby."

"So where's the Omega Link now?" asks Lucas.

"We destroyed it."

What? says Lucas with dismay.

"You never knew this," says the Dark Man, "but the device was actually a two-way link—transmitter as well as receiver. We used it to monitor your actions and plans while you had it."

Lucas is outraged. "You eavesdropped on us?" He stares unbelieving at the Dark Man. "You *spied* on us?"

Jake grins at his brother. "Kind of ironic, isn't it?" he says.

The Dark Man utters a sound that could be a chuckle.

"Ironic, yes," he says. "But we decided that with the

Omega Link compromised, it was best to simply dispose of the device."

"Hey, isn't it amazing how this is *exactly* like *The Lord of the Rings*," says Cyril suddenly, looking around the table.

Everybody just stares at him. A whippoorwill cries as a soul departs. Then a frog croaks ten times.

"Come on, people!" says Cyril. "Think about it. Each race sends a representative to join in a fellowship to save the earth."

Jake rolls his eyes. "Cyril," he says.

"Bear with me here, dog," says Cyril with hushed zest. "I mean, we've got humans, right? You, me. Lucas. Plus a hobbit." He pats Lexi on the head. She whacks his hand away. "Then there's the large folk." He looks at Marco. "Including my man Yeti, representing the Hairmen of the North." Next Cyril points at Mr. Latimer. "And look, the wandering guy: the Ranger!" Mr. Latimer nods back. "And of course, there's also, uh, there's . . . there's Dr. Tim."

"I'm a scientist!" barks Dr. Tim irritably.

"Exactly," says Cyril. "The White Wizard!"

Marco stands up. "Whatever," he says. "Let's go."

"Right," says the Dark Man, rising as well. "There is much to do." He turns to Jake. "This was a courtesy meeting, nothing more. Clearly, since this Omega operative is now contacting *you* and not *us* . . . which I *cannot* understand"—his hands clench into fists—"we must stay in close touch.

But you are still banned from the woods. Understand?"

"Why?" demands Lucas.

"That's none of your business," answers the Dark Man.

"Well hey, maybe the next Omega text message I get will be none of *your* business," says Lucas hotly.

Marco glances at the Dark Man. "Gee," he says. "He's got you there, Brad."

The Dark Man whirls to Marco. "Why do you keep calling me Brad?" he says angrily.

Marco shrugs. Tensely, the Dark Man turns to Lucas. He takes a deep, rattling breath.

"Something is . . . *waking* in the woods," he says. "We don't know what yet. But there can be no doubt: It is *very* dangerous. Stoneship has been the focus of Viper's activities for many months." His shoulders slump a bit. "That much is obvious. We've seen evidence of some sort of gathering."

"*Gathering?*" repeats Jake.

"Yes," says the Dark Man. "Something . . . some *signal* . . . is drawing attention to the woods."

Jake snaps his fingers. "Viper's monsters are returning to the woods. Mr. Latimer saw the Slorg there. We saw the nanoswarm this morning. And Cyril saw the Black Hand beast."

"It *is* dangerous in there," says Marco, looking at Jake. "He's right about that."

Jake nods. "Okay," he says.

Marco turns to the Dark Man. "Isn't there something you wanted to, *ahem* . . . give to the children?"

The Dark Man hesitates a second, then digs his hand into a small black pouch slung over his shoulder. He pulls out a handful of Spy Link headsets and places them on the table.

"Four units," he says.

"Yes!" shouts Lucas.

"Sweet!" cries Lexi.

"Our field frequencies are locked out of these units, of course," says the Dark Man. "But you can communicate with each other and Marco. And we can contact you if necessary." He turns and heads to the front exit, adding, "Which I don't foresee, to be honest."

Marco follows him. "*Adiós*, team," he says.

The huge men hustle out, one after the other: two massive slabs of humanity, squeezing through the shop's front door. As Jake watches them go, it strikes him that maybe Cyril is on to something for once.

The Large Folk.

Next he watches as Mr. Latimer and Dr. Tim exit. *The Ranger and the Wizard*, thinks Jake. Slowly, the world-famous Bixby grin spreads across his face.

It does feel like a "fellowship."[11]

Jake turns to the others: the small folk.

---

11. Look, I know comparing this crew to *The Fellowship of the Ring* is a stretch. Don't blame me; I'm just the author. All I do is write down whatever Cyril says.

"Okay, let's get organized," he says with a wink at his brother.

"Team Spy Gear," says Cyril. "The Extended Edition!"

Everybody laughs at this horribly lame joke.

The sun is setting on the cliffs. The rocks blaze red in the horizontal light.

Amid the buzz of activity around the cave mouth—shouting engineers, the roaring backhoe, the loaders, the churning coaxial rotors of the stealth helicopter—one man stands as if in the eye of a hurricane. He rubs his gloved hands together as he gazes soberly at the figure on a stretcher being hauled past him toward the chopper.

Next to him, a man in mountain fatigues points to the stretcher and says, "That's Gibbs, sir."

"I figured as much," says the Gloved Agent, a little testily. "Will he live?"

"I believe so, sir," says the other man. "We'll chopper him to Samarra, and then airlift him back to D.C. tonight."

"Good," says the Gloved Agent. "And who are you again?"

"Agent Mason, sir," says Agent Mason.

"Ah, yes. Mason."

The Gloved Agent clasps his hands behind his back and raises his head a bit. It's his favorite leadership pose. "And your team leader is where, Mason?" he asks.

"In the cave," says Mason. "Shall we?"

"Yes, let's," says the Gloved Agent.

They wait until the backhoe wheels out of the sloping cave entrance and then they descend into the darkness. Both men flick on powerful Blackhawk Night-Ops Gladius flashlights and follow a path of glowing blue markers down a low rock corridor—so low even the Gloved Agent, a short man, must stoop to walk. After about twenty yards the tunnel-like corridor opens into a large cavern.

"It's over here, sir!" calls a voice.

Mason leads the Gloved Agent toward the voice, which comes from a dark figure silhouetted in front of a bank of glaring xenon spotlights.

"Hello, sir," says the team leader.

"What have we got?" asks the Gloved Agent.

"I hope you're ready for this," says the leader.

A trace of indignation ripples over the Gloved Agent's face. "I assure you I've seen more than you could *possibly* imagine," he says.

"Maybe so, sir," says the leader. "But I'll wager you've never seen anything like *this* before."

He approaches a large tarpaulin spread over something large on the cave floor. Two armed agents stand guard nearby. The leader reaches down and unceremoniously lifts the tarp.

"Good *God!*" gasps the Gloved Agent. "Is it . . . is it alive?"

"No, sir," says the leader. "It was left like this. Abandoned." He drops the tarp back down. "We found the escape tunnel. It leads, as you might suspect, to a VTOL landing pad."

The Gloved Agent is pale. As he tries to speak, he teeters slightly. Mason quickly takes his elbow, but the Gloved Agent yanks it away. As he does so, an angry little squeak escapes his throat.

"I'm fine, Agent Mason, thank you," he says.

"Sorry, sir."

Mason exchanges a quick, amused look with his leader.

"Did you find a laboratory?" asks the Gloved Agent. "Any kind of technology workspace, or storage facility?"

The leader nods. "Yes, sir, we found all of that, and a lot more," he says. "Unfortunately, it's all toast."

The Gloved Agent nods. "Of course," he says.

The three agents stare down at the tarpaulin-covered shape for a few seconds. Then the Gloved Agent whirls away and heads back to the exit tunnel.

"Let me make a preliminary report on this," he says. "Then I'll tour the rest of the facility."

"Yes, sir," calls the leader. "Uh . . . sir?"

The Gloved Agent spins around with a flourish. "Yes?"

"What shall I do with this . . . carcass?"

"Find an industrial-size freezer and get it in there, posthaste!" barks the Gloved Agent.

The leader nods.

As the Gloved Agent follows his flashlight beam out of the cavern, the leader turns to Mason and quietly says, "You heard the man."

Agent Mason nods. "I heard him, sir."

"Posthaste!" barks the leader.

The two agents crack up laughing.

(7)

DOCTOR WHO?

Summer evenings in Carrolton can be as humid as a steam bath—no breeze, and almost no sound. Kids just sit on porches, watching fireflies. This is one of those evenings. The Bixby brothers stroll lazily along Agincourt Drive, waving to occasional neighbors and chatting quietly about the day's events.

Their destination: the Happy Grotto in the Carrolton Soccer Complex.

"So you withheld this information from the Big Boss," says Lucas, grinning.

Jake holds up the manila envelope of photos. "It was a brain lock," he says. "I was so excited about everything, I totally forgot."

Lucas grins at his big brother. "And Barbie Bickle figured it out, eh?"

"She has a sharp eye for detail," says Jake, a little defensively.

"Oh, I have no doubt of that," says Lucas. "Let me see that photo again."

Jake hands him the envelope; Lucas extracts the photo of the rock formation. He pulls a mini-flashlight out of his pocket and trains it on the glossy print.

"Yep," says Lucas, studying it. "That's definitely the Happy Grotto formation. But in Uzbekistan?" He gives Jake a sly look. "Maybe we should keep this little revelation to ourselves."

"No, dude," says Jake. "We share whatever info we've got with the Agency. We're all in this together . . . like it or not."

"Yeah, well, I don't like it," says Lucas, waving the photo. "It just *irritates* me that they won't tell us everything *they* know. They don't even trust us to go back into Stoneship!"

Jake cracks a wry grin. "Well, because we're just, you know . . ." he begins.

"*Children*," finishes Lucas. He snorts. "Yeah, just children . . . children who figured out most of the *flipping* clues in this whole *flipping* Viper affair."

"I share your pain, bro," says Jake. He takes the photo back and slides it into the pack. "But the Dark Man thinks he's protecting us from evil. I guess I can't blame him."

"Whatever," says Lucas. "Try Marco again."

"Okay," says Jake.

Both boys quickly don their Spy Link hands-free headsets; each brother slides a subtle earpiece over one ear and then hooks the base unit onto his belt and switches on the receiver.

"Hey, Marco, this is Jake, are you out there?" calls Jake. "Hello? Dude, there's something I forgot to tell you guys. It might be kind of important. Hello? Hello?"

"Broseph, let *me* call him," says Lucas, eyes bright. Radio-speak is Lucas Bixby's favorite thing going forward into infinity and then back around to the Dawn of Time. So when Jake nods at him, Lucas clears his throat and says, "Ah, roger that, this is Bravo Two[12], calling Mike Romeo, do you read me? Mike Romeo, Mike Romeo, this is Lima Bravo, do you copy, over?"

For a few seconds, all they hear is static.

Then suddenly a very, very loud voice barks WHO IS THAT? in their ears.

Both Bixbys go *"Aaaaaaaagh!"* and rip their Spy Link headsets off their ears. You sound like the Bixbys! roars the voice. What's with all this Shakespeare crap?

"Dr. Tim?" says Jake, holding his earpiece six inches away from his ear. "Is that you?"

Yes! howls Dr. Tim.

"So they gave you a Spy Link too?" asks Jake.

12. "Bravo" is the military alphabet designation for the letter "B" which, here, stands for "Bixby." Lucas is Bravo Two; Jake is Bravo One. "Lucas Bixby" is Lima Bravo; "Jake Bixby" is Juliet Bravo.

Of course they did! blasts Dr. Tim. **I'm a scientist, for God's sake!**

Jake grins. "What's up, Dr. Tim?" he asks, still keeping the earpiece at a good distance.

I've got some good, hard information, some solid data to report, says Dr. Tim. **But nobody seems to be listening except you boys.**

Lucas cautiously slips his headset back over his ear. "Where are you, Dr. Tim?" he asks.

I'm right here! bellows Dr. Tim.

An inconceivably loud car horn unleashes a brain-rattling blast right next to them on the street. Both Bixbys jump ten feet and go *Aaaaaaaagh!* again. They turn to see a big white pickup truck at the curb. The sign on the driver's door reads:

NATIVE CARE SOLUTIONS
ORGANIC LAWN & PEST CONTROL
GIVE DR. TIM A CALL TODAY!

Beneath this lettering is a picture of Dr. Tim wielding a Bolivian machete. He looks more like an insane mass murderer than a lawn guy, to be honest. Under his picture is a line of tiny text that reads: DON'T USE LAWN POISONS . . . OR I'LL BE VERY ANGRY.

That's frightening enough. But even more frightening is the sight of the actual live Dr. Tim directly *above* the sign, glaring out at the Bixbys through the driver's side window. As he prepares to yell again, both boys immediately rip the Spy Link headsets off and jam them into their pockets.

"How are you boys?" he yells with a wave.

"Except for the yellow fluid dripping out of my shattered inner ear, I'm doing just great, Dr. Tim," says Lucas.

"Where are you headed?" asks Dr. Tim.

"Over to the Soccer Complex," answers Jake.

"Hop in," says Dr. Tim. "I'll take you."

The boys jump in the cab and Dr. Tim steers the truck along Agincourt Drive.

"What's your hard data, Dr. Tim, if I may ask?" asks Jake. "Can you tell us?"

"Absolutely," says Dr. Tim. He points at a notebook with a green cover sitting on the dashboard. "Open up to the last page of writing."

Jake grabs the green notebook and flips it open. The so-called writing looks like the scratching of a demented chicken, so Jake turns to Dr. Tim with a quizzical look and asks, "What's it say?"

Dr. Tim gives him a fierce look.

"Last spring," he says, "when I was researching those swimming bugs, I found a scientific article published by a research team investigating reports of amphibious ants around the world. One of the places they explored was in Uzbekistan."

"I remember hearing about that," says Jake, nodding.

"Well, all this talk of Uzbekistan reminded me of that!" shouts Dr. Tim. "And it got me thinking!"

"How so?" asks Jake, covering his ear and wincing in pain.

Dr. Tim steers the truck around a curve in Agincourt Drive. The tall, gated entrance to the Soccer Complex's parking lot is just ahead. Dr. Tim's eyes gleam with luminous intensity.

"Boys, remember those underwater colonies we found on the floor of Carrolton Reservoir?" he asks.

Last spring (as chronicled in Book 5: *The Shrieking Shadow*) Dr. Tim found colonies of amphibious insectlike creatures living in pumpkin-shaped hives on the floor of the reservoir. As it turned out, these "swimming bugs" were actually bits of a super-organism that could combine into larger and larger composite creatures, including the massive black squid-monster that Cyril just saw escaping from Slurry Water Park.

"Those were creepy," says Lucas.

"They were beautiful!" barks Dr. Tim.

Lucas doesn't like insects much. But he nods gamely and says, "Okay. Let's go with that."

Jake says, "Dr. Tim, before Marco left last spring, he told us that scientists found those same underwater hives somewhere in Uzbekistan."

"Correct," says Dr. Tim. He jabs a finger at his notes.

"See? A Russian team found them in a man-made reservoir called Charvak. But the American scientists came up empty in Uzbekistan, according to their published results." Dr. Tim raises his huge white eyebrows. *"Or so I thought."*

Now the intensity in the cab of the truck is so thick you could slice it. Wouldn't it be cool if you could wrap sliced intensity in clear plastic and sell it as "Intensity Bread," or maybe call it an "Intensity Loaf" if for some reason you hate bread or maybe you just like the word "loaf"?

Anyway, what was I talking about?

Oh, yeah . . . Dr. Tim.

As they pull into the Soccer Complex parking lot, Dr. Tim explains how the American report suggested that the trip to Uzbekistan yielded no discoveries of note. But today's meeting in Ye Olde Ice-Cream Shoppe got Dr. Tim thinking about that summary report again. Afterward, Dr. Tim got in touch with some of his government contacts (he used to work at NCAR, the National Center for Atmospheric Research) and he did some more digging.

"I found their real report," says Dr. Tim.

Lucas almost bursts, he's so excited. "It was classified, right?"

Dr. Tim nods vigorously. "By an unnamed agency of the United States government," he says. "Top secret, special intelligence, Umbra classification. Only the highest security clearance can access."

"How did *you* get access?" asks Lucas, wide-eyed.

Dr. Tim grins like a maniac. "I have friends," he says.

"So what did this report say?" asks Jake eagerly.

Dr. Tim parks the truck in the northeast corner of the humongous parking lot. He yanks up the parking brake, then says, "The American team found hive colonies in a subterranean lake connected to a huge cave complex in the Kyrk-Tau region."

"Kyrk-Tau?" gasps Lucas. He looks at Jake. "Isn't that the area where the Agency thinks Viper has a cave hideout?"

"Yep," says Jake. He turns his full attention to Dr. Tim's scrawled notes now. "This cave complex, Dr. Tim . . . is it by any chance linked to a huge cavern called Aman Kutan?"

"That's exactly right," says Dr. Tim.

Back in Book 5 (again), the Dark Man and Marco had briefed Team Spy Gear on this shadowy, cratered region in Uzbekistan. Again, the Agency's suspicion was that Viper's lair was somewhere in Kyrk-Tau, tucked into one of the thousands of grottos, caves, chasms, and clefts gouged from the earth by ancient meteor strikes and countless epochs of erosion.

"What happened to the American scientific team?" asks Lucas.

"Nothing much," says Dr. Tim. "They just came home, split up, and scattered across the country, returning to their work in university labs." He pauses. "Except the project leader."

"What happened to him?" asks Jake.

Dr. Tim gives Jake a grim look. "Dr. Conrad resigned his professorship two weeks after he returned and, well . . . he disappeared."

"Wow," says Jake.

Dr. Tim reaches over and flips a page of his notebook.

"Here's a printed excerpt of the team's report," he says. "Read it!"

The boys read the excerpt stapled on the page. It says that during the cave exploration, Dr. Conrad descended a side tunnel off of the vast Aman Kutan central cavern while tracking a trail of the black insects. He disappeared . . . and didn't return for two full days.

"Wow again," says Jake.

"Yes," says Dr. Tim. "I called one of his colleagues just an hour ago, Dr. Finnegan-Fox. Here's what she said." He points to a circled scrawl of notes.

The notes read as follows: *Says Tom Conrad returned a changed man. "We all certainly concur on that point, if nothing else."*

"Holy cow!" says Lucas.

"It's suspicious, all right," says Dr. Tim. "Dr. Conrad was in the midst of a *big* research project funded by the National Science Foundation. His resignation shocked the school."

"Which school?" asks Jake.

"University of North Carolina," replies Dr. Tim.

Jake and Lucas exchange a look.

"Aren't North Carolina teams called the Tarheels?" says Lucas.

"Hmmm," says Jake. *"Tarheel.* Could be a coincidence."

"Yes, could be," says Lucas.

Then, in brotherly unison, they say: *"Or not."*

Cyril just finished dinner with his parents and he's about to call the Bixbys when his phone rings. He looks at the number and his stomach flutters. Joyfully, he punches the air a couple of times.

Then he answers the phone in his most bored voice.

"Speak to me," he says.

"Get your carcass outside," says Cat.

"Huh?" says Cyril.

"Outside, cowboy," she repeats breathlessly. "I'm standing in front of your house. I just ran, like, a mile to get here."

"Cool," says Cyril.

He snaps the phone shut and heads out his front door. Indeed, Cat Horton stands on his front sidewalk, wheezing and sweaty. She looks great.

"S'up?" says Cyril.

Cat leans over, hands on knees, huffing out ragged breaths. *"Aaaaaaah,"* she says.

Cyril leans over too. "Should I summon qualified medical assistance?" he asks.

"Shut up," she gasps.

After a few seconds, Cat recovers enough to stand up and talk.

"They're going in," she gasps. "Tonight."

"Who?" asks Cyril.

"The Wolf Pack," says Cat.

"Going in where?" asks Cyril.

"Stoneship Woods."

Cyril starts chuckling. "I don't think so," he says.

Cat frowns at him. "Why not?"

Cyril pats her on the shoulder. "Those aren't *health inspectors* at the quarantine checkpoints, my child," he says.

"Everybody knows that," says Cat.

"The minute Brill sets off a motion detector," says Cyril, his voice rising like a Scottish preacher, "the Foul Goons of Mordor shall descend upon him, leaving naught but bones in their wake." He nods his head sadly. "And lo, it will be *most* gruesome."

"They don't plan to set off any motion detectors," says Cat.

"That's impossible," scoffs Cyril. "Those sensors will detect even the slightest movement on the ground around the entire perimeter of the woods."

Cat grabs Cyril's arm. "They're not going in on the

ground, you dogmeat," she says. "They're going in over the top."

"Over the top of what?"

"The Slurry Water Park wall," says Cat. "Wilson told me they figured out a way to get across to the big trees, then crawl through the branches over and past the sensor radius of the detectors. They've been planning it for weeks!"

Cyril looks stricken.

"What else did he say?" he asks.

Cat says, "Something about an access road. He said they found an access road last fall, but something scared them away. This time, they're taking what he called 'precautions.'"

Cyril shakes his head. "Wilson just . . . *told* you all this?"

Cat grins. "The dude loves to brag about Brill's stupid schemes."

"Huh," says Cyril. "Hey, wait. Slurry Water Park closes at six o'clock." He looks at his watch. "That was an hour ago. How can they . . . ?"

"Brill is hiding inside the park," says Cat. "He'll wait until ten p.m., and then let the pack in through an employee entrance. They'll sneak to the west wall in the dark and set their ropes and stuff."

"This is not good," says Cyril.

"Why?" asks Cat.

"That Stoneship access road will take them some-where that, that . . . that they *must not go!*" says Cyril with dismay.

"Hey, I bet they get caught," says Cat with a little laugh. "Really, like you said, they're clumsy goofs. Why worry?" She sits on the porch.

Cyril looks down at his hands.

"Hmmm," he says. "If I tell Jake about this, I know what *he'll* want to do." He looks up at Cat. "You see, our whole team wants to get back into Stoneship too. Every-one, uh . . . except me."

"So don't tell them about Brill's plan," says Cat. "Just go tip off the Health Department goons. That will ensure the pack gets caught."

Cyril clasps his hands tightly. He squeezes them around each other.

Cat sees his distress and stands up again.

"So what do you want to do, soldier?" she asks. She glances at her watch. "We don't have much time."

Cyril sighs.

8:18 p.m. The Happy Grotto. Dr. Tim and the Bixby boys stare at . . . a bunch of rocks.

"There they are," says Lucas, nodding.

"Yep," says Jake, nodding.

Dr. Tim is looking at the Uzbekistan photo. "That's them, all right," he says, nodding.

Everybody nods some more.

Now what?

The 257-acre Soccer Complex feels like a separate county by light of day. But in the dark its boundaries are so far-flung it seems even bigger—more like a medium-size foreign nation. At night, when no games are scheduled, a small army of groundskeepers patrols and grooms its perfectly manicured plains.

The playground rock formation known as the Happy Grotto is next to the parking lot, near the Juggling Green and the trolley station where you can catch a ride via one of three crisscrossing trolley routes through the massive complex.

Lucas turns to Jake. "Yeah, *now what?*" he asks, agreeing with the author for once.

Jake shrugs. He looks at Dr. Tim.

Dr. Tim hands back the photo. "Let's examine these things," he says.

The three guys start crawling around on the rocks. Each one is coated with a spongy, rubbery surface that makes it softer and easier for little kids to scale. The rocks jut up from a sand pit filled with digging implements and plastic playthings. It's truly a Kid Paradise.

But Lucas asks the key question:

"Why would a playground *exactly* replicate an actual rock formation in the remote central mountains of Uzbekistan?"

Jake shrugs. "No idea," he answers.

Something beeps on his belt.

"The Spy Link receiver!" he says. "Somebody's trying to call us."

Both Bixbys slip their headsets back over their ears. As they do so, Jake glances over at Dr. Tim.

"Uh, Dr. Tim, you might want to bend your mouthpiece just a *little* farther away from your mouth," says Jake respectfully. "Your voice is pretty powerful, sir."

"Oh! Okay, Jake," says Dr. Tim, adjusting his set.

As they flip on their receivers, a voice is already talking over the link.

. . . do you read me, over? calls the voice. I repeat, this is Charlie Whiskey, calling Tango Sierra Golf, any of you, are you out there? Jake? Lucas? Spunky the Girl? Helloooooo?

"Bravo Two here, I read you, over," replies Lucas with a calm professional tone.

"Yo, Cyril," says Jake. "We're both here, dude."

Where are you? asks Cyril.

"At the Happy Grotto," says Jake. "Nothing to report yet. We're looking around."

I have some news, says Cyril.

"You sound . . . reluctant," says Jake.

I am, says Cyril.

"About what?" asks Jake.

They hear Cyril sigh loudly. Then he says, Well, I just

got a very disturbing report from Cat. Apparently, the Wolf Pack plans to . . . *WOOOOOOIIIIIIII-AYAYAYAYA!*

"Aaaaagh!" cries Jake, grimacing. "What the donkey is that?"

All three of them are forced to pull off their Spy Link headsets again.

"Some kind of transmission," says Dr. Tim. "A very *powerful* transmission, I might add."

Now they all feel a growing tremor in the very rocks beneath them. It builds slowly, soon vibrating loud enough to be heard without the headsets. The entire rock formation starts pulsing—a powerful, rhythmic pulse. In the Spy Link earpiece it sounds almost like a kettle drum.

THRUMMM! THRUMMM! THRUMMM!

Dr. Tim holds his earpiece close to his ear again.

"It's a radio transmission," he says. "Somebody's sending out a signal."

"What kind of signal?" shouts Lucas over the vibration.

"I don't know," says Dr. Tim. "This structural architecture, though . . . it's familiar." He looks around at the rocks. "It's laid out like a phased array transmitter, the kind you might see on an aircraft carrier for guiding in aircraft. Very powerful."

Now the bigger boulders are throbbing. It's like standing atop a huge subwoofer.

Jake feels a pulse of something else: fear. He turns to Dr. Tim.

"Should we get out of here?" he calls.

"Probably!" shouts Dr. Tim over the growing, deepening pulsation. "I think this entire grotto is some kind of landing beacon."

"For who?" asks Jake.

They all look up into the sky.

8

HUNTER

The mobile field unit parked in the woods is a marvel of modern technology. Right now, Marco's great bulk fills the command center of the Agency's camouflaged all-terrain van. He sits at a fully loaded workstation wearing Koss Noise-Cancelling headphones, head-banging to hip-hop music in the phones as he taps away on a keyboard.

Behind him, a man ducks inside via a low door. He steps up to Marco's back and taps his big shoulder.

Marco spins violently, whipping off his headphones.

"*What now?*" he shouts.

The agent steps back, holding up his hands. "Whoa there," he says.

"Is there something you *want* from me?" asks Marco.

"No, just checking in," says the agent. "Any luck yet?"

"Luck?" says Marco, giving the man a brutal look. "Yeah, I hacked into the database a couple hours ago. I just forgot to tell you about it because I'm chatting with my girlfriend."

The agent smiles. "Just . . . checking in," he repeats, backing to the door.

"Agent Anderson?" calls Marco.

"Yes, Mister Rossi?" replies the agent.

"Don't check in anymore," says Marco.

Anderson nods. "I'll relay that request to my superiors," he says.

"Which is just about *everybody*," murmurs Marco as Agent Anderson closes the door.

Marco is about to put the headphones back on when the door bursts open again. This time the visitor is Marco's equal in stature: the Dark Man. He enters, pointing to the display screen.

"You won't believe this," he says.

Marco quickly spins back to the keyboard. "What do you want up?"

"Go to Field Reports," says the Dark Man. "Open the photo files in AK-101."

Marco clicks a page of thumbnail shots onto the screen. Then he opens the first photo. It shows a picture of what looks like an insect crumpled on its side.

"That's a praying mantis," says Marco.

"A dead mantis," says the Dark Man.

"Dead, yes," says Marco.

The Dark Man looks at Marco. "We just got these from the Aman Kutan site."

"So?" says Marco. "It's a bug."

"Open the next file."

Marco clicks open the next photo in the series. It's so stunning he does a classic double take. "Holy mother of God," he mutters.

"Yes," says the Dark Man.

This photo shows the same praying mantis. But here a man crouches next to the creature. If the picture is to be believed, the insect is actually larger than the man. Much larger.

"How could that be?" asks Marco.

"We're running genetic scans as we speak," says the Dark Man. "I think that we can safely assume that . . ."

Suddenly an alarm tone starts ringing on the display panel. Marco punches a button and a live camera shot appears onscreen. It's an overhead view of a large pumpkin-shaped hive illuminated by banks of red lights in a forest clearing.

The Dark Man puts a finger to the Spy Link earbud in his ear. "We have activity," he says, listening. "Something is happening."

Onscreen, a swarm of black crablike creatures is flowing from a hole on top of the hive. They start swarming over the hive in crisscrossing patterns. Marco gives an involuntary shiver.

"I hate those things," he says.

"What triggered this?" asks the Dark Man quietly.

Marco looks over at some other readouts on the console. "This is interesting," he says. "Look. Sensors are getting pounded by some kind of signal. See?" He points to a fluctuating LED light. "It's a pretty rhythmic pulse. And it must be very close by."

The Dark Man rips off his Spy Gear headset. "It's overpowering the field frequencies," he says. "I can't hear a thing."

"Wow," says Marco. "You're right. Something's happening." He points at the onscreen hive scene, where the crawling crab creatures now flow in perfect, orderly spirals around and around the hive colony. "And those guys were the first to know."

As the Bixbys and Dr. Tim back away from the pulsating Happy Grotto, Jake notices a quick movement about fifty feet away, over by the fence that separates the Soccer Complex from Stoneship Woods. He looks closer. A dark figure is lurking.

Jake leans to his brother's ear.

"Dude, do you still have that Night Scope you stashed?" he says quietly.

"Of course I do," replies Lucas. "I never go anywhere at night without it. Why would I? Why would anyone? I mean, it's totally nuts to go out into the dark without night-vision capability. Only a dog-brained fool would attempt such a thing."

"Okay, okay," says Jake. "Chill."

At the end of the Shrieking Shadow adventure, the Dark Man confiscated all of the amazing spy gadgetry that Team Spy Gear had been using to fight evil and so forth. But Lucas, who was personally devastated by this act of piracy, managed to sneak off with a couple of mini-gadgets plus one full-size Spy Night Scope, a set of slick night-vision binoculars.

"Put the scope over there," says Jake, nodding subtly toward the fence. "I saw something move."

Lucas slips the binoculars out of a side pocket of his cargo shorts and quickly trains them on the spot.

"It's The Kid!" he whispers. Through the scope, Lucas sees the hooded intruder react to being spotted. "He knows I see him! Wow! There he goes!"

As Jake starts to run toward the spot, Lucas watches The Kid turn and scale the eight-foot-tall chain-link fence. His speed is stunning—indeed, he climbs like a human spider. When he reaches the top, he goes over headfirst . . . and clambers inverted down the other side. That's right: He climbs down headfirst!

"That's amazing!" says Lucas.

When he reaches the ground, The Kid glances back quickly, then runs off into the trees. His stride is very low to the ground—so low it looks like he's skating. By the time Jake reaches the fence, The Kid has disappeared into Stoneship.

"Forget it, man!" shouts Lucas. "He's gone!"

As he watches Jake skid to a halt at the fence, Lucas hears Dr. Tim step up beside him.

"Who is it?" asks Dr. Tim.

"Just some kid in a hood," says Lucas.

"Ah," says Dr. Tim. "Must be Bobby."

"Bobby?" says Lucas, lowering the Night Scope and turning to the scientist.

"Was he wearing a black hood?" asks Dr. Tim.

"Yes!" says Lucas.

"That's Bobby," says Dr. Tim. He glances over at the rock formation. "Listen!"

The rhythmic pulse drops to a low, barely detectable vibration. Then it just stops. Jake comes jogging back from the fence. All three peek up at the sky again. Then Dr. Tim shakes his head.

"Very strange," he says.

Lucas turns to Jake. "Dr. Tim says The Kid's name is Bobby," he says.

Jake turns to Dr. Tim. "You *know* him?"

"Not really," he says. "I worked on their lawn when they moved in."

"At his house on Agincourt Drive?" asks Jake.

Dr. Tim nods. "Yes, and the Hunters are nice folks. They *hate* lawn poisons. My kind of people." He scratches his stubbly white beard. "That Bobby is a strange one though."

"How so?" asks Jake.

"Never talks." Dr. Tim turns and starts for his truck. "Never see his face."

Lucas watches him go, frowning. After a few seconds he calls, "Did you say his last name was Hunter?"

"Yes!" barks Dr. Tim over his shoulder.

Lucas and Jake exchange a look.

"Hunter," says Lucas.

Jake nods. "Could be a coincidence," he says.

Then in unison both boys say: *"Or not!"*

They're about to follow Dr. Tim back to his truck when Jake's cell phone rings. Jake looks at the incoming number, then slaps his forehead. "It's Cyril!"

Oh yeah, Cyril. The Bixbys were talking to him via Spy Link right before the Happy Grotto started pulsating and wrecking on the transmission, remember?

"Hey," says Jake as he flips open the phone. "Sorry, dog, we got cut off before."

"What was that ghastly sound?" asks Cyril.

Jake quickly recounts what happened and adds, "Let's go back to Spy Link so we can all talk."

"Roger that," says Cyril. Seconds later, the Bixbys are linked and they hear Cyril say, Can you read me, Bixbys? Hello?

"We read you, Charlie Whiskey," says Lucas. "Over."

So you guys think "Contact Hunter" in the Omega message refers to The Kid? says Cyril. He hoots out a Cyrillian laugh. That certainly sounds just wacky enough to be true.

"Dude, *nothing* would surprise me at this point," agrees Jake.

Oh, yeah? says Cyril. Well . . . how about this?

And here Cyril lays out the whole Wolf Pack plan to infiltrate Stoneship via the water park. When he finishes, there is a stunned silence all around.

Finally, Lucas manages to speak. "Holy flipping codfish," he murmurs. "That plan is *entirely workable*."

I had to breathe into a paper bag when I heard it, admits Cyril. It completely and utterly destroys my sense of order in the universe.

Yes, I know it strains the bounds of credulity, but Brill Joseph's plan is actually . . . *a good plan*. Hey, even brain-damaged lemurs make good decisions once in a while, if only by accident.

Now Jake recovers enough to say, "Guys, we've got to follow them in."

I knew you'd say that, moans Cyril.

Hey, guys! calls a voice over the link.

"Lexter Lopezsky!" says Lucas. "Dude! So karate's finally over. How was it?"

Lexi has just started taking karate lessons this summer. The idea of Lexi Lopez with a third-degree black belt

should strike fear into the hearts of evildoers everywhere, of course. But for now, it's just another scheduled
activity (on top of gymnastics and ballet) that makes
Lexi crazy.

I don't want to talk about it, she answers.

"Well, buck up, ninja," says Lucas. "You won't believe
what's going down tonight. Where are you?"

The mall, says Lexi glumly. She hates the mall. With
my mom, she adds. I gave her that letter from Marco while
we were eating at the Food Court. After a pause she says,
Mom's still crying.

Dr. Tim's truck horn unleashes a quick blast. Jake
waves at the driver. "Let's go, Lucas. Cyril, are you at
home?"

Yes, boss, replies Cyril.

"We'll be there in five," says Jake.

"Lexi, can you head to Cyril's?" says Lucas.

You bet, she says.

Suddenly, Jake's cell phone rings. "Who's this?" he
says, eyeing the incoming number. "I don't know this
one." He flips open the phone. "Hello?"

"Bixby," says a girl's voice.

Jake is stunned. "Barbie?" he says.

"Yeah . . . and, uh, you might want to get over here
fairly quickly," she says.

"To your house?" asks Jake.

"Yes, Bixby," says Barbie. "My house."

Jake is speechless. Then: "Did something happen?"

"You might say that," says Barbie.

"Like . . . what?" asks Jake.

"Like twelve guys in black cars just busted into the house next door," says Barbie.

8:47 p.m. Dr. Tim parks his truck, lights off, just around the bend from Barbie Bickle's house. Jake and Lucas leap out, thank Dr. Tim and, staying low, scamper through several front yards to Barbie's house. As they approach her front yard they note three black sedans parked on the street.

"Wow," says Lucas. "Serious stuff."

Now both Bixbys hear loud static over their Spy Link headsets.

"Cyril?" calls Jake. "Lexi? Are you there?"

Static rattles in his ear. It gets louder as they creep toward a side gate to Barbie's backyard. Lucas flips open his cell phone and punches a speed-dial button. Nothing happens.

"Dude, our cell phones are knocked out too," he says, frowning.

"There's some kind of powerful interference here," says Jake. "I don't like this."

A few seconds later, the gate swings open.

"Come on!" says Barbie quietly. "I tried to call you again, but my phone's dead."

She leads the boys around the corner of the house and across the backyard to the opposite fence, the tall one between her yard and The Kid's. Jake can hear movement and deep male voices speaking in hushed tones on the other side.

He leans close to Barbie's ear and whispers, "I need to see over. Do you have a ladder?"

Barbie seems short of breath for a second, but then she inhales deeply and whispers, "Yes, but it's not very tall." She looks up at the fence. "It might work."

She points to a small stepladder leaning against a small gardening shed. Jake quietly retrieves it and sets it up by the privacy fence. The ladder has only three steps; when Jake reaches the top step he still can't quite see over.

Lucas springs into action. He digs into one of his cargo shorts pockets.

"Try this, bro," he whispers.

He hands up a Micro Periscope. Jake extends the viewing scope to its full six-inch length—just long enough to extend above the top of the fence. Then he puts the eyepiece to his eye and surveys the scene in The Kid's backyard.

And what he sees is, well . . . surprising.

Because except for all the guys in black swarming the area, The Kid's backyard looks pretty normal.

There is indeed a swimming pool—a big circular one,

glowing aqua in the night. Multicolored patio lights in silver housings are installed at regular intervals around the pool's perimeter.

Two agents jiggle the door handle of a cabana, a small pool hut. Another man has his arm elbow-deep in the pool; he pulls out a sample container filled with water, which he caps. Several others walk around with what appear to be radiation detectors. These men wave metallic wands attached by cables to small, handheld units with glowing digital readouts. A group of five agents stand near the back door of the house, consulting quietly.

Jake frowns: *What's going on?*

He steps off the ladder and huddles with Lucas. Barbie leans in close too.

"Wow, you smell good!" whispers Lucas to Barbie.

Barbie seems perplexed. "Me?" she asks.

"Yeah, you," says Lucas, nodding. "What is that . . . like, jasmine?"

"Good nose, Bixby," says Barbie.

"Cool," says Lucas. He turns to Jake. "So what's up, bro?"

Jake stares at his little brother with his mouth half open. Then he just shakes his head.

"What are they doing?" asks Barbie.

Jake gazes at her. "Well, it's a pretty serious sensor sweep of the area," he says. "They're taking samples and so forth."

Now they hear another vehicle pull up in front of the house. Car doors burst open and then slam shut. The kids listen as footsteps click up the driveway and into the backyard, just on the other side of the fence. Jake is about to climb the stepladder again for a peek when he hears a deep, familiar voice.

"Give me an escort detail," says the voice. "I want at least six of you with this detainee. And get me a chopper, Anderson. *Now.*"

"Yes, sir," answers an agent.

Lucas whacks Jake's arm. "It's Dark Man!" he whispers excitedly.

"But sir, I'll have to go down the street to call in transport," says Agent Anderson. "Something's disrupting our com-link here. A fairly powerful magnetic field, it looks like, from our scanners."

As Jake steps up the short ladder he hears another familiar voice.

"I don't think he's dangerous," says Marco.

"I didn't say he was," replies the Dark Man.

"In fact," says Marco, "I think he wants to help somehow."

"I just want him safe, and in a secure, controlled facility," says the Dark Man.

Jake peers over the top of the privacy fence. Just below him stand the two large men, surrounded by a squad of agents. Between Marco and the Dark Man, looking light and lithe as a monkey, is none other than the small hooded figure of The Kid—or, if Dr. Tim was correct about his name, Bobby Hunter.

In a flash, Jake knows what he must do.

That's right—it's a classic Jake Bixby moment.

Without hesitation he jumps up, locking his arms and resting his elbows on top of the fence. Then he scoots over, hangs by the top for a second, and finally drops down behind the shocked-looking cadre of agents. Several drop into a ready crouch.

"Oh, look," says Marco, without a trace of surprise. "It's a Bixby."

Jake grins. "Howdy, fellas," he says. He raises his palms to the nearby agents. "I'm unarmed, except for the Swiss Army knife in my back pocket."

The Dark Man folds his arms. Jake hears a half chuckle escape the man's LP voice-filter mask.

"I don't suppose you're alone," says the Dark Man.

Now Lucas struggles over the top of the fence with some difficulty. As he hangs down, Marco grabs his waist and lowers him gently.

"We Bixbys tend to stick together," says Lucas.

"Yes, I know," says the Dark Man.

Jake faces the small figure next to them. The Kid is short, maybe two or three inches shorter than Jake. The opening in his hood is as black as coal smoke. It's a very odd phenomenon; Jake can make out no features whatsoever in the hood's darkness.

"Are you Hunter?" asks Jake.

"Hunter?" echoes the Dark Man.

Marco looks stunned, and then nods. "Of course," he says.

Something about The Kid's reaction strikes Jake; he looks incredibly wary and alert. Although the stranger gives no response, nor makes any kind of gesture at all, Jake feels like he's received an answer.

"Omega told us to contact you," says Jake.

The Kid—Hunter—now turns fully toward Jake.

Jake says, "He gave us a pass code: Tarheel."

Lucas steps up next to his brother. "Does that mean anything to you?" he asks.

For a few seconds, nobody moves. Then, slowly, The Kid reaches a hand into the hip pocket of his loose black pants. When he pulls the hand out, it is curled in a fist, wrapped tightly around something. He turns his head in a slow swivel, stopping it at each person standing in the circle around him, as if examining them—scanning them, even. After he completes this scan, he turns to Marco and reaches out his closed fist.

Marco looks at Jake.

"He's giving you something, dude," says Jake.

"Why me?" asks Marco.

Jake shrugs. "He sees something in you, I guess," he says.

"Take it!" says Lucas, excited.

Marco reaches out his hand. Hunter opens his, and a shiny object drops into Marco's. Then, with amazing agility, Hunter slides sideways through the ring of agents and dives into the aqua pool.

"Stop him!" shouts the Dark Man.

Several agents leap fully clothed into the water and lunge for the hooded figure floating just under the pool's surface. But Jake watches in amazement as something very strange happens.

First, a dark fluid seeps from Hunter's body. At first Jake thinks it's blood, but no—it's black like heavy oil, not red. It swirls downward through the water, leaving behind the body, which floats limply like a rag doll. Two agents haul the body out of the pool, but it is clearly now an empty vessel.

Second, the multicolor spotlights around the pool start to flash and pulse. Then, slowly, the housings begin to rotate. The lights swivel so that the beams all shoot directly into the pool water.

Third, a loud hum indicates some large mechanism is at work. Soon enough, the source is clear; the very floor of the aqua pool is moving! It slides into the pool wall to reveal a large underwater compartment holding a round, metallic-silver shape. Distorted a bit as seen through the

113

water, it appears to be about the size of a large automobile. As the last of the pool floor disappears into the wall, the silver craft starts to rise.

Jake can see that it is rotating slowly. Multicolored globe lights flicker on around its edge.

"I don't believe it," he says.

"It looks like Viper's craft!" says Lucas. "Only it's . . . different." Aghast, he turns to his brother. "Do you think he's Viper?"

"No," says Jake. "No, I don't. But . . . there's obviously some connection."

Nearby, the Dark Man is barking into his Spy Link mouthpiece.

"Get Charlie One in here *now!*" he shouts. "And call in all available air support."

"It's too late," says Marco next to him.

Now the spinning craft breaks the surface of the water. The pool spotlights stay trained on the circular ship, following it as it rises. Then, with no warning, the craft tilts slightly and zips away so fast it almost seems to disappear into thin air.

Jake stares at the spot where it had been hovering, wondering: *Did we just let Viper escape?*

HAVING A BALL

9:22 p.m. Cyril and Lexi sit on the front porch of Cyril's house, waiting.

Where are the Bixbys? They're supposed to be here by now. Remember, the Wolf Pack is making its move on Stoneship at ten o'clock. Time is running short. So is Lexi. (Ha! That's a joke.)

"You're in a grim mood there, Spunky," says Cyril. "Is karate that repugnant?"

"No," she says.

"So karate's good, then?"

"No," she says.

"Then what else is wrong?" says Cyril. "Speak."

"Nothing."

"You lie," says Cyril.

Lexi doesn't respond.

The fact is: Lexi Lopez is a world-class daredevil. But she hasn't done anything dangerous during this entire book. This makes her cranky, and frankly, kind of angry at the author. Indeed, so far today, she hasn't done much of *anything*, spy wise.

Cyril puts his finger to his Spy Link earpiece.

"Hey guys?" he calls into the mouthpiece. "Jake? Lucas? Please respond. We need Bixbyness, over."

Nothing but silence, except for a little static.

"Great," says Cyril.

Now he checks his phone. No messages, no missed calls. Dang!

Lexi watches this. "Why do you keep checking your phone, like, every ten seconds?" she asks crankily. "Jake said to use the Spy Link."

"I'm expecting another call," says Cyril.

"From who?" asks Lexi.

"None of your business," replies Cyril.

Lexi just looks at him.

"Okay, well, if you're going to *harass* me like that," says Cyril, "Cat's supposed to call." He leans his elbows on his bony knees. "She went to go spy on the Wolf Pack. She said she'd call me the moment they start mobilizing for their water park caper. I'm getting a little worried, that's all. So get off my case, will you? And stop yelling at me. I know I *look* like a tough guy, but I've got feelings too." Cyril starts sobbing theatrically. *"Oh, just forget I said anything!"*

Lexi rolls her eyes. But a little grin spreads across her face.

Cyril's phone starts vibrating in his hand.

"Aha!" he shouts. "At last!" He glances at the phone. "Hmmm, it's a text message." Then he frowns. "Wait. This is from an 'Unknown Caller.'"

Lexi sits up, suddenly very alert. "It's him again!" she says.

Cyril says, "Who?"

"Omega!" She jumps up and peers over Cyril's shoulder at his phone.

"Why would he contact me?" asks Cyril.

"Maybe he can't get through to Jake or Lucas," says Lexi.

Cyril gives her a look. He says, "Or maybe Omega knows who the *real* boss is on this team."

"Me?" says Lexi.

"*Yes, you!*" shouts Cyril.

Cyril clicks open the text message. It reads: BEACON ENTRY: BUCKYBALL. ABORT CODE HOLOGRAM: 32F - 90E + 60V = 2. OMEGA.

"Good God," says Cyril, staring at the message. "The guy's a total nerd."

"Buckyball?" says Lexi.

Cyril just shakes his head. "Clearly he's lost his marbles," he says.

"Why is there *math* in the message?" asks Lexi.

"This is how nerds communicate," explains Cyril. "I know this because I'm a nerd."

He saves the text in his phone. Then he tries to call Jake, but gets a CONNECTION FAILED message. Same thing happens with Lucas.

He jumps to his feet. "Okay, let's go," he says.

Lexi frowns up at him. "Where?"

"Upstairs," says Cyril.

"Why?"

"Do you know what a buckyball is?" asks Cyril.

"No," says Lexi a little defensively.

Cyril gives her a parental look. "Well, then, we'd better do some *research*, shouldn't we?"

9:38 p.m. The mobile field unit, with its forward satellite antenna deployed, looks like a black rhino hunkered on the street between Stoneship Woods and Carlos Santana Middle School.

Inside, Marco sits at the workstation console; Jake Bixby stands behind him, peering past Marco's wild hair at the main monitor. A small crystalline cube sits on the control panel next to the keyboard. This is the shiny object that Hunter dropped into Marco's hand before he jumped into the pool and, uh, *seeped* down to his flying craft.

Lucas sits nearby, gawking at all the high-tech electronic equipment lining the walls.

"This is *deeply* acceptable," he says. His eyes sparkle like live wires. "I want this."

"I'll make sure Brad *gives* it to you when this Viper case is closed," says Marco.

Jake grins. "Dude, is his name really Brad?"

"No," says Marco.

Jake shakes his head. "Hard to believe we're *still* banned from the woods."

"Don't feel so bad," says Marco. "So am I."

"You're kidding!"

"Nope." Marco taps in a few commands. "They have a very tight lid on that colony. They want none of what they call 'surveillance variables.'"

Jake is stunned. "Colony?" he repeats. "You mean that big hive we saw in the woods last spring?"[13]

"Correct," says Marco.

Lucas looks queasy. "I thought they were going to exterminate those black bugs," he says.

"Certain Agency science experts wouldn't allow it," says Marco.

"Why not?" asks Lucas.

Marco taps a few keys. "I guess they decided that additional study might help reveal Viper's master plan." He barks out a quick laugh.

Jake points to something onscreen. "Look," he says.

---

13. Yes, this is yet another reference to stuff that happened in Book 5: *The Shrieking Shadow*. If you haven't read that book yet, perhaps you should just go play with some pond scum.

"Yes, the cube's emitting a wireless signal," says Marco, leaning forward now. "Fascinating." The intensity of his typing goes up a notch. Then, suddenly, the screen flashes bright white. "Wow, it's flowing right into a default graphics program," says Marco. "It's self-configuring! Holy crap. Look at that."

A series of 3-D shapes begin popping onto the screen, one by one. Each one appears and then starts rotating. Some of the shapes are recognizable: simple geometric figures like spheres and cubes. Then come rows of trees, flowers, birds and other animals, houses, footballs, soccer balls, chairs, lamps, and a few generic human shapes. But other objects are very alien-looking. Some appear to be . . . well, creatures.

"Look there," says Jake, tapping the screen. "That looks like the Black Hand creature." He points at other similar shapes. "See? That one looks like the squid-thing Cyril described."

"Yes, it does," says Marco, nodding.

"But what does it mean?" asks Lucas. "What are all these shapes for?" He looks at Marco. "Why would Hunter give us this thing?"

"I have no idea," says Marco.

Jake's cell phone rings. "Aha!" he says, looking at it. "It's Cyril. We've got service again." He flips open the phone and says, "Yo, dog."

"I'm here, as always, woofing the woof," replies Cyril. "Can we all get on the link now?"

"Sure," says Jake. "We had some interference earlier." He nods at Marco and Lucas. "Let's link up."

9:44 p.m. Back in Cyril's Bedroom, Cyril and Lexi sit on stools in front of Cyril's computer, a monstrous desktop rig.

Both kids listen over the Spy Link as the Bixbys describe the Hunter incident, including the part about the oily essence leaving Hunter's body and flying off in a craft like Viper's.

"Dude, wait a minute," says Cyril. "You're saying that Hunter might be . . . *an intelligent fluid?*" He barks out a sharp laugh. "That's beautiful, man!"

Well, whatever he is, he isn't human, says Jake. Not like anyone we know, anyway. With the possible exception of Mrs. Kite over on Willow Road.[14] Honestly, I think we're dealing with something that's very, uh . . .

"Alien?" says Cyril eagerly.

Jake sighs over the link. I guess, he says.

Cyril beams. He has long proposed that alien life-forms exist among us. Frankly, just one look at his hair would confirm that for anyone. But now Cyril has some news in return.

"Guys, we got another text message from Omega," he says.

What? exclaims Lucas. When?

14. As I pointed out long ago in Book 2 of this series, most Carrolton kids believe that Mrs. Kite is actually a massive eyeball on a stalk.

"About fifteen minutes ago," says Cyril. "It came to my phone. He probably tried your phones first, but couldn't get through, so . . ."

What's it say? interrupts Marco with a hint of urgency in his voice. **Read it.**

Cyril exchanges a look with Lexi. "Okay," he says. "If you insist." And then he reads the odd text message from Omega: "Beacon entry: BUCKYBALL—that's all in caps, by the way. Abort code hologram: thirty-two F minus ninety E plus sixty V equals two. Omega."

There is a long silence over the Spy Link. Finally, Jake says, **Cyril. Come on.**

"What?" says Cyril.

Stop goofing with us.

"I goof you not," says Cyril. "That's the message, Jake. Right, girl?"

"That's the message," confirms Lexi.

There is another silence. Then Lucas says: **Buckyball?**

"Well, by golly, that had me stumped too," says Cyril. "So guess what? I did a little Googling."

Jake laughs. **That's our Cyril,** he says.

"Okay, this is wild," says Cyril. He clicks open a window on his computer screen. "A buckyball is actually a sixty-atom carbon molecule discovered by three American chemists—a discovery so *interesting*, apparently, that these dudes won the 1996 Nobel Prize in Chemistry."

Wong, you said the word 'buckyball' was capitalized in the text message, right? says Marco.

"Correct," says Cyril.

To me, that indicates a code word, says Marco. An entry code.

"A *beacon* entry code," says Cyril. "Especially since the word 'buckyball' comes after the words 'beacon entry,' followed by a colon."

Right, says Marco.

A beacon entry code, repeats Lucas. You know, Dr. Tim thinks the Happy Grotto is some kind of radio beacon. He thinks it was sending out a signal.

So if you can link into the beacon frequency, maybe you just type BUCKYBALL to enter the beacon software, says Jake.

Maybe, says Marco.

Then you can use the beacon to send a signal, adds Jake. But what signal?

There is another silence as everybody ponders these possibilities for a few moments.

Then Cyril says, "Uh, my buckyball research report wasn't quite done yet."

"He has more," says Lexi.

Okay, says Jake. Lay it on us.

"The second part of the message," says Cyril. "Okay, I don't know what 'Abort code hologram' means, but the equation after it is actually the mathematical formula for

a buckyball. Now hang with me here; it seems complicated, but it's not, really."

"It's amazing," chirps Lexi.

Cyril bows to her. Then he continues: "A buckyball is,
like, a bunch of polygon shapes fused together and
wrapped around a sphere. Its formula actually refers to
these shapes, their faces, edges, and vertices: 'thirty-two F
minus ninety E plus sixty V equals two.'"

Dude, you're losing me, says Jake.

"Hang on," says Cyril. "Trust me, all will be clear.
Twelve of these thirty-two shapes around the sphere are
five-sided figures—you know, pentagons. The other
twenty faces are hexagons, or six-sided figures. Again,
you fuse these thirty-two polygons together into a pattern that forms a sphere."

Okay, now I'm totally lost, says Jake.

Cyril winks at Lexi.

"Jake, *think hard*, my man," he says. "A sphere . . . made
entirely of pentagons and hexagons? Does this not ring a
bell with you? *You*, of all people?"

There is yet another pause.

And then Jake blurts out: Great flying monkeys!

Back in the van, Jake leans over and grabs the mouse
from Marco's hand. He uses it to scroll down the rows of
3-D holograms being broadcast by the crystal cube onto
the workstation screen.

"Fellas, do you know what a buckyball looks like?" he says, grinning.

Marco and Lucas look bewildered. Jake keeps scrolling until he brings up a row of sports-related shapes: balls, goal posts, hockey sticks, etc. Then he double-clicks on the rotating hologram of a soccer ball.

"A soccer ball?" says Lucas.

That's right, grasshopper, says Cyril over the Spy Link. A soccer ball has the same mathematical formula as a buckyball—the Nobel Prize–winning, 60-carbon fullerene molecule.

"This is a coded message," says Marco, staring at the soccer ball.

"How so?" asks Jake.

"After you gain access to the radio beacon," says Marco, "you input this hologram to trigger an abort message of some sort. In other words, you transmit this soccer ball, and the signal tells somebody out there to forget the plan. Abort mission. Get it?"

Now Lucas stares hard at the slowly spinning ball.

"But who's getting the message?" he asks. "And what mission are they aborting?" His cell phone abruptly beeps. He whips it open excitedly. "Another text message," he says. "Unknown caller."

"Omega again?" asks Jake.

Lucas reads the new message out loud: "It says, 'Bring

the Hunter to landing site. Omega.'" Lucas looks up at Jake. "Bring *the* Hunter?"

Maybe the Hunter is hunting Viper, says Lexi via link.

Jake, Lucas, and Marco exchange looks. Then all three start to smile.

"Lopez," says Marco. "Sometimes being related to you isn't half as bad as it could be."

Thanks, says Lexi.

Marco looks at Jake. "It would be comforting to know that someone with actual brains is hunting Viper too."

"Maybe he's, like, an alien bounty hunter!" says Lucas. "Or a sheriff or something!"

Yes, says Cyril. **Patrolling the galaxy in a water bottle, pouring himself on bad guys.**

Jake looks at Lucas and asks, "The message says something about a landing site, right?"

Lucas flips open his phone again and punches a button to check the text. "Yep," he says.

"So who's landing?" asks Jake, looking around.

My guess is an alien invasion fleet, says Cyril.

Marco shakes his head. "Wong, you continue to astound me," he says.

In what way?

"In a bad way," says Marco.

"And where would this landing site be located?" muses Jake.

"My guess: somewhere in Stoneship," says Marco.

Hey guys, I'm getting a call from Cat, says Cyril. **This probably means the Wolf Pack is making its move on the water park. So are we in on this action, or are we not?**

Jake warily looks at Marco.

"Dude, I know you said it's dangerous in the woods," he says. "But we might have found a way to sneak into Stoneship—like, past the guards and motion detectors and stuff."

Marco gives him a skeptical look. "No way," he says.

Jake nods. "Way," he says.

Marco thinks for a moment. Then he looks up at Jake from his chair. "Whose plan is it?" he asks.

Jake is uncomfortable. "Well, uh, there's this guy named, uh, Brill Joseph and . . ." he begins.

"That kid's an *idiot*," says Marco.

"Well, yes," admits Jake. "But he actually has . . . a good plan." He winces as he says this.

Guys, Cat says we have about five minutes to get to the park's employee entrance, says Cyril. **So what is it? Yea or nay?**

Jake and Lucas look at Marco.

"So what do you think?" asks Jake.

Marco glances at the rotating soccer ball on the main monitor.

"Okay," he says.

"*Yes!*" shouts Lucas. "To Stoneship!" He can't help but hop a few times.

"Bixby, you're rocking the van," says Marco.

"Oh, sorry," says Lucas.

Marco turns to Jake. "I'll hack the beacon signal and figure out this abort code issue, but I'll also monitor your progress from here," he says. "Don't make any stupid moves."

"Don't worry," says Jake with a grin. "We'll leave stupidity to the Wolf Pack."

"We'd better hurry," says Lucas.

Yes! Hurry! cries Cyril. **It's almost ten!**

"We're on our way!" calls Jake.

We're leaving now too, says Lexi with excitement. **Cyril, I think we'd better run fast or we won't make it in time.**

"Yes, it should be close," says Lucas, checking his watch. "But I think we can get there before it's too late!"

Hurry, Team Spy Gear! Hurry!

⑩

CHUTES AND LADDERS

10:14 p.m. Outside Slurry Water Park.

Yes, it's Team Spy Gear . . . *in action, at last!* Ha! Finally! No more stupid math formulas!

Look! The Bixbys, Cyril, and Lexi all crouch behind a purple Triceratops[15] outside the employee entrance to Slurry Water Park. They wait silently in concealment. It's very hushed and . . . well, a few night things chirp and whisper. So actually, it's not *perfectly* silent. But it's close. And did we mention yet that the team is concealed and also hiding? Well, let's mention it again to kill some time.

Uh . . . what time was it again? Oh, yeah. It's now 10:15 p.m.

Then, slowly, it becomes . . . 10:16 p.m.

---

15. Is anything more pathetic than a purple dinosaur? Hint: The correct answer is pronounced "No."

Hmmm. It's getting harder for the author to maintain the suspense here, kids.

"Okay, where are they?" demands Lexi loudly.

"Shhhh!" hisses Cyril. "We must be silent as we wait here, waiting and waiting for something, for *anything* to happen." He throws a rock at the author. "Even a *mistake* would be good."

Jake taps his fingers restlessly on the dinosaur's left haunch. "So . . . let's go over the plan again," he says. "Maybe a couple of times."

Lucas is snoring on the ground. Cyril reaches down and shakes him. Lucas gasps and spits, looks around sleepily, and mumbles, "Is it tomorrow night?"

"We're reviewing the plan again," says Lexi, knitting a shawl.

"Oh," says Lucas. "Okay. So . . . when the last Wolf Pack guy goes through the door, Lexi runs to the doorway and slides a piece of bark into the doorjamb so the door doesn't close completely and lock. Lexi, do you have the bark?"

Lexi moves the Afghan[16,17,18] she just knitted and holds up a flat piece of bark.

16. No, Lexi didn't knit a citizen of Afghanistan. An "Afghan" here is a blanket, wrap, or shawl of colored wool, knitted in geometric shapes.

17. An "Afghan" is also a citizen of Afghanistan, of course. But Lexi didn't knit a human being from Afghanistan. No, she knitted a blanket, wrap, or shawl of colored wool, knitted in geometric shapes.

18. Actually, Lexi *didn't* knit a blanket, wrap, or shawl of colored wool, knitted in geometric shapes. She didn't knit anything. This "knitting" is just a plot device to kill some more time. Apparently it's working, because you seem to be reading all of these ridiculous footnotes.

"Good," says Lucas, lying back down. "Now please don't wake me until something happens."

Look, guys, the fact is: Spying isn't all action and fun and running and getting goose bumps. A lot of spying time is spent in concealment, waiting. Frankly, it's boring. Plus you spend a lot of time talking and figuring out clues and whatnot, *yakkity yakkity*, like in the last chapter.

Wait! *Did you hear that?*

Somebody's coming!

Whew! Yes, that snarfling and grunting and yipping and whining are sure signs that the Carrolton Wolf Pack is on the prowl. Here they come! Yes, within minutes, hostile shadows begin to dart and zigzag to and fro across Slurry's parking lot, moving toward the Employee Entrance door, more or less.

Cyril watches in horror. "This could take *hours*," he says.

Then Jake hears the employee door rattling.

"That must be Brill," he says. "Here we go, people!"

Lexi creeps around the side of the dinosaur, piece of bark in hand.

Now several boys emerge from the darkness into the pale pool of light from a security lantern hung directly above the door. Wilson Wills is in the lead, and nine or ten other wolves follow him. They're dressed in black, with long sleeves and cuffs, plus black stocking caps pulled low. Wilson has a coil of heavy-looking cable slung over his shoulder. Another boy carries a big sack.

When Wilson reaches the door, he knocks on it—the rapping rhythm is clearly a code.

The door opens.

Brill Joseph stands there, eyes glowing red.

Flames rise behind him. Demons howl in agony. Okay, I'm overdoing the action a bit here, mostly to make up for all the boring stuff earlier. But trust me, Brill's a scary guy.

"Let's go!" he snarls. "Move!"

Wilson and the black-garbed wolves file in quickly. As they do, Lexi tenses, ready to sprint. When the last guy hustles through the doorway, Brill snarls and steps outside. He looks both ways, snarling. Then, snarling, he steps back inside.

Timing her rush perfectly, Lexi bursts out from behind the dinosaur.

SLAM!

The door slams shut so fast that it exceeds the speed of light and goes backward in time. By the time Lexi reaches it, the door is actually *younger* than when it started to close.

Lexi skids to a halt, holding her pathetic piece of bark.

"Wow," she says. "That closed *really* fast."

The other Team Spy Gear members step out from hiding and approach the door. They stare at it.

Cyril nods. He claps Lucas on the shoulder.

"Good plan," he says. "I have to say, I really admired it, despite its failure."

Lucas approaches the door and places his hand on the knob. It doesn't budge.

"Crap!" he shouts.

Cyril steps up next to him. "Locked!" he says. "Wouldn't you know it?" He looks around. "Guess we'd better head home."

Suddenly the door clunks and swings open.

Team Spy Gear freezes. A kid in black stands in the open doorway.

"Let's go, slugs," says the kid.

Cyril's eyes widen. "Cat?" he says.

Indeed, the kid is Cat in disguise. "Hurry," she says. "Brill just told us that security guards check this door every fifteen minutes."

The team rushes in. Cat whips off her black stocking cap; her dark hair spills out. She has a small backpack strapped over her shoulders. She grabs Cyril by the arm and hurries along beside him.

"Slick, eh?" she says.

"Nice work," says Cyril in admiration.

Cat grins, looking exhilarated. "This way," she says, veering off to the left. "Wow, this is fun!"

Cat leads the team up a dark walkway past several popular rides. The computerized water-cycling system is turned off, of course, so no water flows right now. The team passes a twisted maze of hyper-acceleration tubes called "The Brainsucker!" Next they pass the "Foam of Rage!" river rides. And finally . . . the infamous "Ride Where You Just Fall Off a Tower!"

Cyril, in the lead with Cat, halts and holds up his hand.

"There's the pack!" he whispers.

"Oh my gosh," says Lucas. "They're actually going for it."

Just up the walkway slope, dark figures clamber up stairs to a high platform near the park wall. This is the most hair-raising, horrifying water experience of all—the one and only "Senseless Cannon Shot!" Here, each rider leaps into a massive water howitzer, which then blasts you and about forty gallons of water through the air in a shrieking arc until you hit the Tsunami Pool about fifty yards away. There, massive tidal waves rise and hurl you across the pool, flinging you into a narrow chute where four metric tons of water pressure stuffs you into a corkscrew tube that accelerates you at Olympic bobsled speeds until you shoot out into The Big Flush, a gigantic plexiglass bowl of swirling water that swishes you around a hundred times until you finally get sucked through the bottom spigot, which spits you out onto a conveyor belt that dumps you directly into an insane asylum. The entire ride lasts approximately fourteen seconds.

But Brill and company clearly have other plans for the water howitzer.

Several wolves tug hard on the big tublike cannon, swiveling it around so it aims over the back wall. Just beyond the wall, the massive branches of a towering pin oak tree loom darkly. This is the tree at the edge of Stoneship Woods. Wilson hands one end of his cable to Brill, who clamps it on to a high strut supporting the platform's roof. Then Wilson jumps into the water howitzer, holding the cable's other end.

"He's fearless," whispers Lucas in awe.

"And shockingly stupid," adds Cat.

Now Brill steps to the control booth. He barks out something inaudible.

"What's he doing?" asks Jake.

Cat says, "Apparently, Brill asked one of the high school kids who works here how the controls work."

Suddenly, the howitzer discharges.

Encased in a massive water ball, Wilson soars over the wall.

"Note how his burbling shriek of terror recedes as he accelerates away from us," says Cyril, smiling big. "A nice demonstration of the Doppler effect."

The steel cable now runs from the platform out into the matrix of pin oak branches. It hangs slack at first, but then, slowly, it grows taut.

"Incredible," says Jake. "He's alive."

"I have new respect for these guys," says Lucas.

Now Brill starts dispensing gadgets from the big

sack. Each boy gets a small handle and a pulley wheel. The first boy sits the groove of the wheel on top of the steel cable, then clips his handle onto the pulley. Then he grabs the handle and, with a running start, jumps off the platform! Hanging onto the handle, he rides the pulley along the cable over the wall, across the road, and into the big tree across the road—a do-it-yourself zip-line!

Team Spy Gear has to fight the urge to burst into wild applause.

"Wow," says Lexi.

"It's beautiful," agrees Cyril.

Everyone watches as the wolves ride one by one down the zip-line until only Brill is left. After a quick look around the platform, he hooks up and goes too.

"Let's go!" says Lucas.

"Wait a minute," says Jake. "How can we ride the zip-line if we don't have . . . ?"

Cat whips off her backpack and jabs it at him.

"A few guys chickened out," she says. "Wilson had plenty of extras."

Jake opens the pack and pulls out four handle-and-pulley sets.

"Only four?" he says.

Cat nods. "*I'm* not going in there," she says.

"Come on, let's stay on their tail," calls Lucas.

The team plus Cat jab step quickly up the stairs to the

platform. There, Lucas pulls out his Spy Night Scope binoculars and scans the tree across the road.

"There goes Brill," he says. "He's down . . . and off he goes. The coast is clear."

"I'll go first," says Jake.

Lexi jumps in front of him. "Oh no, you won't," she says fiercely.

Jake sees the look in her eyes.

"Right," he says with a grin. "Sorry. I don't know what I was thinking." He steps back.

Lexi slaps the pulley over the cable, clips the handle onto the pulley, grabs on, and runs like a wild animal off the platform. In seconds, she rolls into the high branches of the pin oak across the way.

She looks around, feeling nothing but pure joy and rapture.

"There is *nothing* better than this," she says to herself.

Five minutes later, Team Spy Gear is on the floor of Stoneship Woods.

⑪

A GIRL POSSESSED

Stoneship Woods at night is always fun, especially in the summertime. Darkness brings foul odors and the wet, ripping sound of flesh peeled from bones. In the deepest thickets, rare parasites burst from flowers and burrow into passing meat (*i.e.*, you).

Tonight, Jake leads the way down the Stoneship access road. Behind him, his brother speaks quietly into his Spy Link mouthpiece.

"Okay, Mike Romeo," says Lucas. "We're in. Repeat, we are in the water, over."

Roger that, replies Marco over the link.

"Moving upstream to Point Sierra," says Lucas. "Will keep you advised, over."

Be cool, says Marco. **Out.**

Jake grins over at Lucas. They know the Agency has

access to the open Spy Link frequency, so Marco and the kids have worked out a simple code to keep their illegal Stoneship excursion a secret.

Jake moves lightly up the access road, stopping every few seconds to listen for the yips and howls of the Wolf Pack up ahead. This forgotten, overgrown delivery lane leads to the abandoned Stoneship Toys warehouse, which of course isn't really a toy warehouse at all but a high-tech surveillance post. Team Spy Gear's discovery of this facility nearly one year ago got this whole crazy Spy Gear Adventure series going in the first place. So please don't blame me. If the Bixbys had just minded their own business, I wouldn't have been forced to write these six nutty books against my will.

As the team rounds a sharp bend, Jake hears a tiny flutter. Then he gets a sudden chill.

"Do you feel that?" he says.

Lexi moves up beside him. "That cold?" she asks.

"Yes!" says Jake. "You feel it?"

She shivers. "Yeah."

Jake trusts his instincts, so he stops. He surveys the gnarled trees that reach over the road like great grasping wraiths. A full moon hangs in the sky, casting a sickly glow on things.

Cyril and Lucas move up next to him now, too.

"Do you hear that?" whispers Cyril.

Jake listens for a second. He hears a faint murmur,

almost like a whisper. He looks around at his team; the sound seems to come from somewhere in their midst. "I hear it," he says.

"Now I hear it too," says Lucas.

"It's like *right here*," says Lexi, waving her hand in front of her.

Now they all start turning in circles, trying to pinpoint where the creepy, whispering sigh is coming from. Is it a ghost? Then Jake glances down. A low whirlpool of mist is circling around their feet, barely visible in the moonlight. He grabs Lexi and Lucas and pulls them quickly away. Cyril follows, backing away from the mist.

"What is it?" he says.

Jake's eyes flare with alarm. "A nanoswarm, I think," he says.

As they back away, the whirlpool gathers into a tighter, darker spiral. Its whisper rises in volume to a hiss, almost like radio static. The entity bounces up and down a few times. It looks almost . . . playful.

"You know, it doesn't seem too hostile," says Lucas.

As if in response, the swarm's particles flash silver a few times, sparkling like tossed glitter. Then it changes its spiral pattern. Glowing silver rings pulse up and down its length.

"Wow," says Lexi.

"Awesome," says Lucas.

"It's beautiful," agrees Jake.

"We're doomed," says Cyril. The others look at him. He shrugs. "I'm a pessimist," he says.

Suddenly, heavy footsteps kick through the underbrush all around them. The nanoswarm collapses straight to the ground, hiding in the dust of the road. Branches crack and break as ten large boys in black burst from the trees and surround the team.

The largest one, Brill Joseph, raises his head and howls. The others howl too.

"Uh, Mike Romeo, dude, we have a situation," says Jake quickly into his Spy Link.

Is it bad? replies Marco. I can call backup, but then you'll have to be, ah, extracted from the stream.

"Gotcha," says Jake. "Hold off, but stay tuned."

Will do, says Marco.

Brill points at Jake. "Shut up when I'm talking to you," he says.

Jake takes a step toward Brill.

"What was that, Brill?" he asks. "I didn't understand. Maybe you should take the rocks out of your mouth before you speak."

"Shut up, [censored]!" shouts Brill.

"*Excellent* comeback, Brill," says Cyril. "You wrecked him good, man." He nods. "I see no possible recovery for my colleague."

Cyril's retort draws growls and whines and barking

chatter from the surrounding pack. The smell of blood is in the air.

"Why are you following us?" snarls Brill.

"Yeah!" barks Wilson, who steps up beside his glorious leader.

Jake starts to speak, but then notices something past Brill's shoulder, down the road. Two red points of light glow in the distance. Now they grow larger. Something is approaching.

A large dark figure takes shape around the red eyes.

"Brill," says Jake quietly. "Something is coming."

"*I said shut up, Bixby!*" screams Brill.

"Look behind you, dude," says Jake, backing away.

Brill, of course, refuses to be taken in by this Obvious Bixby Ruse. But some of his minions glance nervously down the road. Before they have a chance to react to the rapidly approaching shape, it unleashes a bloodcurdling shriek. It sounds like a cross between a cougar and the catapult-assisted takeoff of an F/A-18 Hornet from the flight deck of the USS *Abraham Lincoln*. Yeah, it's really loud.

The Wolf Pack breaks ranks and sprints away. So do Jake, Lucas, and Cyril.

But Lexi stands her ground.

"Sit!" she cries at the beast, raising her right hand.

The creature—and yes, I'm sure you've guessed by now that it's the Slorg—halts just a few feet from Lexi. It snarls ferociously at her. Interestingly, though, this snarling is quite oddly enunciated—that is, it almost sounds like the monster is trying to speak but can't because, well, it's a monster with a gazillion fangs in its mouth.

The Team Spy Gear boys halt in their tracks and turn back.

"Lexi, what the dog's name are you doing?" shouts Lucas.

"Sit!" yells Lexi.

And the Slorg sits. No kidding: It sits.

Totally exhilarated, Lexi spins to face the returning boys. The Slorg begins to snarl in its weird articulated way again.

"Son of a Nordic moose," says Cyril. "I think the dog is trying to speak."

"It's more of a cat, really," says Lucas, examining the creature up close.

The Slorg howls and slams one of its powerful, clawed paws on the ground. *Thooom!*

"Careful," says Jake. "Don't get too close."

"It's *frustrated*," says Lexi. "It's trying to tell us something, but it can't." She steps close to the beast. "What is it, boy? What are you saying?"

The Slorg quiets, staring at her with its chilling red eyes. Jake notices a black film wash over their red glow, darkening it. He frowns. Then the creature starts to gag.

It slumps forward, hacking and coughing.

A thick, dark, syrupy fluid pours out of its nose, mouth, and eyes.

"It's dying!" screams Lexi.

Before Jake can react she dives onto the Slorg, cradling its huge limp head in her arms. As she does so, the dark fluid puddles on the ground. Then, with stunning speed, the liquid flows up Lexi's legs and torso, like a fungus creeping in fast motion.

Lucas dives for Lexi.

"No!" he screams.

Lexi tries to struggle, but the black oil reaches her face in a split second. As she wraps her arms around her head, the oil disappears.

She falls to the ground, face-forward.

Lucas and Jake quickly flip her onto her back. Her eyes are closed but her face looks . . . perfectly fine. She's breathing.

"Lexi?" calls Lucas, choked with sudden tears.

Lexi's eyes burst open.

Her eyeballs are completely black.

Back in the "Black Rhino," Marco listens with growing alarm over the Spy Link as the Slorg incident unfolds.

"Bixby?" he calls. "Yo! Are you there?"

He hears gasps over the link. It's inside her head, says Lucas. He sounds like he's in shock.

Marco leaps to his feet in fury.

"What's going on?" he shouts into his mouthpiece.

Suddenly, alarms start wailing. Marco hears engines roar just outside. He peeks out the rear window and sees several "Health Department" vehicles scream past with emergency lights flashing on their dashboards.

We have intruders on the east perimeter! barks a deep voice over the console speakers. All units scramble to the access road exit. And no, Agent Anderson, this is not a drill.

Another male voice comes on breathlessly.

I'm counting eight, maybe ten . . . uh, looks like . . . kids, he says. Yeah. Ten kids. Wow, they look scared.

Great, says another voice.

There is a pause. Then . . . Marco hears Lexi's voice over his Spy Link headset.

We must hurry, she says.

"Hey, kid!" calls Marco. "Talk to me, cousin. Are you okay?"

Do you have the code? she asks.

"Bixby, what's going on?" says Marco urgently. "She sounds messed up."

It's not her, says Jake.

"What?"

Something is . . . talking through her, says Jake.

"Who is?"

Do you have the code, Marco? repeats Lexi's voice. The code I gave you?

Marco's eyes widen. "Hunter?" he says.

Yes.

Marco grits his teeth. "Are you hurting her?" he asks.

No, answers Hunter through Lexi. **Do you have the code I gave you?**

"Yes, I have the code," replies Marco testily.

Listen carefully, then, says Hunter/Lexi. **They are coming.**

"Who?" asks Marco. "Who's coming?"

The Clan, answers Hunter. **If we allow them to land, you will face grave danger. All of you.**

Marco is stunned speechless for a second. Then he asks, "Is this Clan hostile?"

Yes, very hostile, says Hunter.

"Is it Viper's Clan?"

Yes, it is.

"Are you sure?"

There is a pause. Then: **I have been hunting this Clan for several hundred million quanta.**

Cyril says, **That sounds like . . . a really long time, oil man.**

Yes, says Hunter.

Crap! says Lucas. **The Slorg's waking up.**

It is no threat, says Hunter calmly. **In fact, I sensed that the creature has very positive feelings toward you.**

Cyril starts laughing. **This is completely wackified!** he says.

Marco says, "Hunter, how do we stop this Clan landing?"

The abort code, says Lexi, I mean, Hunter.

"The soccer ball hologram," says Marco. "What does it do?"

It signals that this planet is not habitable, says Hunter. **The Clan will leave, and never return.**

Sweet! says Lucas.

"But how do I find the beacon signal?" asks Marco. "I've been looking for hours. Where is it?"

It is accessible only when active, says Hunter.

"So I have to wait until Viper turns it on again?" asks Marco.

Yes.

"Will that be soon?"

Yes, it will be soon, says Hunter. **Very, very soon.**

Marco is about to ask another question when loud interference shatters the Spy Link transmission. A signal detector on the console panel lights up.

"Aha!" says Marco, ripping off the headset. "There it is. Viper's firing up the beacon."

As he reaches for the keyboard at the control console, the van starts rocking—first gently, then violently. Losing his balance, Marco crashes to the floor.

"What the heck?" he says.

As he tries to stand up, a large black tentacle smashes through the back door window. Another one curls in from the van's front, buckling the control panel of the console.

The interior lights go out.

Marco struggles in darkness.

Jake, Lucas, and Cyril immediately tear off their Spy Link headsets, all wincing in pain. Lexi just stands there, unmoving.

"This sound amplification is most distressing," she says.

"Take off your headset, or you'll hurt her ears!" cries Lucas.

"Yes, of course," says either Hunter/Lexi or Lexi/Hunter, depending on whether you flip heads or tails. She removes her headset and holds it up.

Jake points at it. "That sound is the signal beacon, right? Viper is contacting his Clan!"

"It is activated," says Hunter. "He has prepared his host creatures."

"Host creatures?" says Lucas. "Like, creatures that his Clan can live inside . . . just like you inside Lexi, right?"

"Right," says Hunter.

Lucas slaps his forehead. "The Nest!" he shouts. "The bugs! He's breeding amphibious creatures for his Clan to live in!"

Hunter nods slowly. "They would be good vessels on this water planet," she says.

"Let's go!" says Jake urgently. "Our Spy Link is worthless until that beacon signal ends. We've got to find somebody from the Agency and tell them what's going down, and quickly." He looks at Lucas. "Let's hope Marco is inputting that abort code, right now."

Suddenly the nanoswarm pops back up from the dust, sparkling like a fresh snowfall.

"Oh, sure, *now* you reappear," says Cyril, pointing at it.

Jake ignores it and starts running down the access road toward the warehouse. Lucas seizes Lexi's hand and pulls her along too, with Cyril close behind. The nanoswarm follows them. And after a grunt and a shake of its huge head, so does the Slorg.

Lucas glances back over his shoulder as he jogs.

"Dudes," he says, grinning, "we have backup."

Marco rolls out of the van just in time to see it crumple. A gargantuan black squid-creature, big as a house, wraps itself completely around the vehicle and proceeds to crush it.

"Okay, somebody's playing nasty now," murmurs Marco, watching.

The squid unleashes a piercing shriek. It releases the van and lumbers ponderously toward Stoneship Woods, hurling its massive limbs forward and then pulling itself along the ground.

But then it stops. It sits there for a few seconds, as if . . . thinking.

It shrieks again.

The crystal! thinks Marco.

He takes a step toward the van but it's too late. The squid whips two tentacles—each one thirty feet long and thick as a tree trunk—back around the van. Then the beast drags the crushed vehicle behind it as it hurls itself into the trees.

In a few seconds, the shrieking squid and the van are gone.

"This is bad," says Marco.

He turns and starts running up the road, in the direction the speeding "Health Department" cars were heading earlier. And let's stop calling them "Health Department" cars, shall we? They're *Agency* cars, as we've all known since the moment we saw them.

As he runs, Marco whips out his cell phone.

BACK IN THE SADDLE

Team Spy Gear plus "friends"—a sparkling tornado, a slobbering beast, and a liquid—hustle through the main gate of the Stoneship Toys compound. Directly ahead of them, the large main door to the warehouse is wide open. There's no sign of any Agency personnel.

"Wow, good security," says Lucas with a hint of disgust.

"Well, it's good for *us*, anyway," says Jake as he approaches the main door. "If the control room is still operational, maybe we can patch into the Agency's field frequency."

"Why would we do that?" asks Cyril.

Jake says, "We need to contact Dark Man and tell him what's up." He stops and glances up at the sky. "And what might be coming."

Lucas puts his Spy Link earplug to his ear. The Happy

Grotto radio signal is still pulsing loudly. He says, "What if this signal is blocking everything?"

As if in answer, Jake's cell phone rings.

"Ha!" says Jake. "Satellite cellular is working here. We must be far enough away." He looks at his phone. "And it's Marco!" He flips it open and says, "Hey man, did you transmit the abort code?"

He listens for a few seconds, his face growing more and more disturbed.

"Uh-oh," says Cyril, watching him. "I hate that look."

Jake says, "Did you say . . . a *squid*?" He stops at the warehouse door as he listens to Marco's terrifying tale. "It took *the van*?"

"Okay, that's bad," says Lucas.

"Nor is it good," says Cyril.

Now Jake turns to Lexi/Hunter. "Do you have another crystal with the soccer ball hologram?"

"No," says Hunter.

Cyril snaps his fingers. "Wait! We have the formula!"

Lucas looks at him. "So?" he says.

Cyril pats Lucas on the cheek. "Scooter, if there's one thing I can do, it's math. What self-respecting nerd couldn't plot a hologram from a polyhedral formula?"

Lexi nods jerkily. "That is possible and I find it to be an impressive path of reasoning," she says.

Cyril bows. "Thank you, man of fluid," he says.

"Marco," says Jake into his phone. "Cyril thinks he can

re-create the hologram from the formula. We'll give it a shot from HQ. We're here now." He listens for a second, then says, "Okay, good luck to you too. Out."

He clacks the phone shut. Then he looks around at his team.

"Guys," he says. "It's up to us."

Cyril steps forward. "I'm ready to save the world, Jake."

Jake grins. "Me too."

They step inside the main door. A raised control room, suspended from the ceiling to their left, looks out over the warehouse floor. Recessed rungs run up the wall to an open hatch on the bottom of the raised room.

"Who goes there?" calls a voice through the hatch.

"Oh, great," says Jake.

A man's head appears in the open hatch. "Who's there?"

Jake steps forward and waves up. "Hello!" he calls. "It's just . . . some kids."

"Yes," calls Cyril. "Small children, mostly."

"Hi!" adds Lucas in a high voice, waving. "This is neat! You, uh, you wouldn't have a *computer* up there, would you?"

The man quickly swings his legs to the wall rungs and starts climbing down.

"Agent Robinson!" he shouts. "It's the Bixbys!" The kids hear more footsteps pound across the control room above them.

"Great, they *know* us," says Jake.

"I'll get us up there," says Lucas.

He grabs Lexi's hand again and tugs her back outside; Jake and Cyril follow. Then Lucas stands behind the Slorg.

"This entity will protect you," says Hunter.

"How do you know?" gasps Cyril. He looks at Lexi and then says, "Oh, snap. I guess you have . . . *insider* knowledge. Heh, heh."

The first agent flies through the doorway. Seeing the Slorg, he skids to a halt.

"Uh . . . *Robinson?*" he calls.

The Slorg's growl is so deep and powerful it sounds like rolling thunder.

The second agent, Robinson, slides through the doorway and then goes, *"Crap!"*

"If you value your *flesh*, you might want to back away, guys," says Lucas.

The two agents back away.

"Can you control that thing?" asks Agent Robinson.

"Nope," says Lucas.

Jake shrugs. "Sorry," he says.

"That dang dog has a mind of its own," says Cyril.

"It's a cat," says Lucas.

"It's a dog."

"Cat! Come on, look at his eyes."

"Totally dog."

The Slorg unleashes a howl that could melt the clearcoat off a Honda.

Both agents freeze in fright.

"*Yeah*, baby," says Cyril. "And check out my man the tornado too." He looks around. "Hmmm," he says. "I guess the coward is hiding again."

The swarm pops up right next to him, hissing. Cyril jumps.

"Stop doing that!" he says.

Agent Robinson eyes the Slorg and says, "Listen. We've just been authorized to escort you to . . ."

"We're not going *anywhere*," interrupts Jake. "We need your workstation, now."

Agent Robinson rolls his eyes. "Yeah, well, if I could *finish*," he says.

"Oh," says Jake. "Sorry."

"We're supposed to take you up to the workstation," says Robinson. "Delta Leader is giving you priority status Alpha." He looks irritated. "He also wants us to . . . stay out of your way."

The Slorg takes a snarling, hostile step toward the agents.

"And trust me, I have no problem with that," adds Agent Robinson quickly.

Lucas dares to pat the Slorg's back. "He won't actually attack, will he?" he asks, concerned.

"No," says Hunter. "The creature, as engineered, is incapable of harming sentient life."

The two agents visibly relax.

The Slorg suddenly plops down on the ground next to

Lexi. The beast starts panting, its pink tongue lolling out between its massive fangs.

"See?" says Cyril to Lucas. "It's a dog."

Then the Slorg starts licking its paws.

Lucas grins. "It's a cat," he says.

"Come on, guys," says Jake. "We have an alien landing to abort."

He leads the team past the agents in the doorway.

By the time Marco veers left onto County Road 44 and jogs to the Stoneship access road, everyone is gone—no cars or agents, no Wolf Pack boys, nothing. Deserted!

"Perfect," says Marco.

He whips out his cell phone again. He's about to hit his "Jake Bixby" speed-dial button when he hears something rustling in nearby underbrush.

"Hello?" he calls out.

A man emerges from the darkness of the tree line. His long, scraggly gray hair reflects the moonlight.

"I'm Dr. Thomaier Conrad," he calls back.

Marco is stunned. "Dr. Conrad?"

"You probably know me now as . . . Omega," says the old man, pushing unsteadily through the tall prairie grass at the forest's edge. He stops and suffers a short coughing fit.

Marco hurries to help the older man. "How did you get here?" he asks, guiding him up to the road's shoulder.

"With Viper," says Dr. Conrad, breathing heavily. "Excuse me, I am weak."

"Viper's here?" says Marco.

"Yes," says the old man. "For the landing, of course."

"Of course."

Dr. Conrad peers at Marco. "You seem somewhat distressed."

"Yeah, well, I just almost got crushed by four tons of calamari," says Marco.

Dr. Conrad hacks out a few more rattling coughs.

"You don't sound good, either," says Marco.

Conrad waves a hand, coughing. When he finally stops, his voice is a rasp. "I've been living in caves . . . for almost five years," he manages to say. He begins to wheeze and gasp.

Marco waits. When the man finally regains his breath, Marco asks, "Are you alone?"

"Yes," gasps Dr. Conrad.

"How did you get away?" asks Marco.

"I'll show you," says Dr. Conrad, seizing Marco's arm. He bends over, coughing again, then gagging. As he does, he leans his forehead on Marco's shoulder.

Frowning, Marco supports the old man.

Then he feels something warm flowing up his arm.

Cyril swivels side to side in the black leather captain's chair at the workstation console in the Stoneship control room.

"I missed this sweet thing," he says.

Behind him, Lucas runs his hands lovingly over spy gadgets lined up on a set of shelves. He sighs. "They haven't lost any of their splendor," he says.

Something beeps on the control panel; an LED light flashes. "Aha!" says Cyril, leaning forward. "Finally! We are powered up and ready to rock, Houston."

A big central monitor flickers to life over the junction of the L-shaped console. So do four side monitors. These display live infrared video feeds from various field mini-cams planted out in the woods. One shows a wide shot of the clearing where a huge insect hive sits like a massive, mutant pumpkin. The area looks deserted.

"Hey," says Cyril, pointing at this feed. "Where is everyone?"

Another beep: The field frequency locks in. Suddenly, excited voices crackle through the console speakers.

". . . *hundreds* of them!" cries a voice.

"They're coming up through the ground!" shouts another. "Good God, there, see it? It's huge . . ."

"All units pull back! Pull back!"

Now the Dark Man's voice, easily recognizable, rattles in the speakers. "Establish a perimeter, fifty yards," he orders. He sounds remarkably tense. "If necessary, we'll nuke it."

"An air strike?"

"Yes," replies the Dark Man. "Agent Briggs, contact

General Bridger immediately. Get the 447th Tactical Wing in the air."

"Clearly, they've burrowed underground from the hive, sir," calls another voice.

"And how did we miss *that* activity?" thunders the Dark Man. "A *million dollars* worth of sensors around that hive, and they just *dig themselves half a mile to a children's playground?*"

Jake and Lucas exchange a look. "The bugs dug their way to Happy Grotto," says Jake.

"So it's not just a beacon," says Lucas.

Jake nods. "It's the landing site."

"Amphibious creatures, gathering and ready for their new masters," says Cyril. "Right here in Carrolton. Imagine that."

Both Bixbys look at Cyril.

"Okay," says Cyril, flexing his fingers. "Let's scare them away, shall we?"

"Yes," says Jake. "Let's build a soccer ball."

Mr. Latimer has done a lot of driving and watching since this afternoon's meeting at Ye Olde Ice-Cream Shoppe—a meeting that seems like weeks ago, so much has happened since. His job, as he understood it, is to keep an eye on the neighborhoods around Stoneship Woods, and call someone if anything really strange happens. So far, nothing has qualified as "strange."

But now, as he trolls his blue Toyota Avalon slowly

along Stoneship's southern edge, Mr. Latimer thinks he might see his first "strange" thing.

Up ahead, a man with gray, stringy hair crawls down the center line of Ridgeview Drive.

"That's strange," says Mr. Latimer.

He pulls up carefully next to the old fellow and leans out the car window.

"Are you homeless too?" he asks.

The crawling man, of course, is Dr. Thomaier Conrad. He rolls over to a sitting position and tries to talk, but at first it sounds like he's gargling. He clears his throat with loud hacking sounds. He spits. Then he tries to speak again.

"We must get into the forest," says Dr. Conrad weakly.

"Why?" asks Mr. Latimer.

"I fear something bad is about to befall us," says Dr. Conrad.

"You and me?" asks Mr. Latimer.

"All of us," says Dr. Conrad.

Mr. Latimer hops out of his Toyota and helps the old man into his front passenger seat. Then he runs around the car, hops back in the driver's seat, and starts driving.

"What bad thing is happening in there?" asks Mr. Latimer as he turns left onto County Road 44.

Dr. Conrad doesn't answer directly. He holds his head, rubs his temples, and says, "Perhaps there's something I can do to stop it. After all, I know him better than anyone."

"Who?" asks Mr. Latimer.

"Viper," replies Dr. Conrad.

Mr. Latimer pulls over near the old Stoneship access road. He turns hard to shine his headlights on the row of tall oaks blocking the old entrance. "I'm told there's a road here," says Mr. Latimer. "Some say it leads deep into the woods."

"We must try," says Dr. Conrad. "I must reach the Hunter." He jabs a hand into his pocket and pulls out an object. He holds it up: a small crystal cube. "He needs this."

"I don't see how we can," says Mr. Latimer. But then he notices a thicket of saplings to the left of the tall strong oaks. He points at the spindly young trees. "*There*, maybe. We might get through there. But it would surely cause considerable damage to my car."

"I'm worried about those boys," says Dr. Conrad.

"Boys?" repeats Mr. Latimer. "What boys?"

"The Bixbys," says Dr. Conrad.

Mr. Latimer turns to the older man. "The *Bixbys* are in there?" he asks sharply.

"Yes."

"Right now?"

"Yes, and I fear they're in grave danger."

Mr. Latimer guns his car over the asphalt curb of County Road 44 with a sickening *Thunk!* Without stopping, he aims at the saplings and stomps the Toyota's accelerator to the floor.

(13)

VIPER AT LAST

Okay, so who needs a crystal cube when Cyril Wong is such a fricking genius?[19]

It took him fourteen seconds to find a freeware 3-D polygon plotter, then another sixty-six seconds to plug in Omega's formula to create a 3-D soccer ball, and then dump the mesh hologram file into a 3-D design program. Here he colored the pentagons black and the hexagons white.

(If you want to see what Cyril's final hologram looks like, go stare at a good old-fashioned black-and-white soccer ball.)

Next, Cyril hacked into the radio beacon's transmitter with a free online radio software toolkit, using it to track the

---

19. He paid me thirty dollars to write this.

powerful signal's gateway and then something with gremlins and a magic wand. (Look, I have no clue what Cyril did and he was just a little too busy to explain it all to me.)

Once he intercepted the beacon frequency, he found an encryption screen blocking entrance to the transmitter software. Cyril typed in the code "BUCKYBALL" and got immediate access to the transmission. Near the bottom he found a box labeled "Abort Code Field." He dumped in the 3-D soccer ball file and clicked the onscreen Transmit button. The beacon started transmitting the hologram out into space.

This final step happened five seconds ago.

Now everybody in the room is cheering and slapping Cyril's back.

"Dude, that was *wicked* smart," says Jake.

"Unbelievable," says Lucas, shaking his head. "I'm in total awe, dog."

Lexi walks up to Cyril.

"Can I look?" she asks.

Cyril grins at her. "At what?"

"The telemetry," says Lexi/Hunter.

"Sure!" says Cyril. "I have no idea what that means, but it's all yours." He rises from the captain's chair. Lexi takes his place and starts typing faster than human fingers can possibly move.

"Hmmm," says Hunter. "I sense that she is perplexed by this experience."

Lucas leans down and looks into Lexi's eyes. "So she's *awake* in there?" he asks.

"Not exactly," says Hunter. "But she will have some memory of these events."

Lines and lines of incredibly complex-looking code suddenly appear onscreen and start scrolling upward at ridiculous speed. The code characters are very alien. Lexi watches intently.

"Holy cow," says Lucas. "Are you *reading* that?"

"Yes," says Hunter, eyes jittering.

"What is it?"

"Readouts from your laughably primitive human satellite sensor grid," she says.

"Sweet!" says Lucas. "What do they say?"

After a few more seconds Lexi smiles. It is a very crooked, freaky smile, and her face twitches oddly a few times, but frankly, it's one of the best-looking smiles Mankind has ever seen. Here's why:

"They're gone," she says.

"The Clan?" asks Jake.

"Yes," says Hunter. "The fleet departed."

Jake is stunned. "So quickly?"

"Yes," says Hunter. "Their capital ships, which simulate asteroids in form and movement, will be many parsecs away, very soon." She turns to Cyril. "You have saved your world from brutal enslavement. I commend you."

For once, Cyril is speechless. He just smiles like a mop-headed goofball.

Downstairs, the Slorg begins to snarl loudly.

"Uh-oh," says Lucas. "I hope Rover's not terrorizing the guys again."

"Come on, let's go call him off," says Jake.

Cyril kneels next to the captain's chair, grinning like a mad scientist. "Teach me how to read this satellite telemetry, o great fluid one," he says to Lexi.

"I'll try," says Hunter through Lexi. "But your brain is most likely too small."

Jake hoots at this and heads for the floor hatch.

"Coming, Agent Robinson!" he calls down.

But when the Bixbys descend the wall rungs, they find the Slorg snarling ferociously at Marco in the doorway. Robinson and the other agent appear to be asleep in a nearby corner.

Marco just stares at the beast. There is absolutely no trace of fear in his eyes.

Jake grins. "Impressive, dude," he says.

Marco's eyes turn to Jake. They remain totally expressionless.

Now Jake frowns. "You okay, Marco?" he asks.

The Slorg's growls and yaps are getting almost frantic. Lucas takes a step toward the beast. "Hey, hey!" he calls. He claps his hands a couple of times. "Chill, boy! It's okay. Marco's cool. He's with us."

Marco twitches and raises his hands.

The Slorg yelps in pain. It starts writhing on the ground.

Frowning, Jake stares at Marco. "What are you doing, man?"

Tremors ripple across Marco's face. It's a frightening effect. After a few more seconds, the Slorg scrambles past Marco out the door. It lopes off howling into the night.

Then Marco turns to Jake.

"Finally," he says. His voice is a rasp.

Jake shakes his head. "Finally what?" he asks.

"You are Jake Bixby, yes?" says Marco. "And so we meet at last."

Jake and Lucas exchange a perplexed look.

Suddenly, they hear glass shattering, and Cyril hollering. The Bixbys look up to see a very pale-looking Cyril slide through the ceiling hatch and then scramble down the rungs.

"Jiminy jacks!" he exclaims. "Did you see that?"

"See what?" asks Lucas. "Where's Lexi?"

Cyril sprints across the warehouse floor. "There she goes!" he shouts. "Out the south door!" He spins back to Lucas. "She tossed the chair through the plate glass and jumped out!"

"What?" cries Lucas.

"It was sick!" says Cyril. "She snagged the freaking

loading crane, shimmied along the ceiling track, crawled headfirst down the wall, and ran out the south door." He shakes his head. "Guys, it raises beastliness an entire order of magnitude." He glances toward the main door-way. "Oh, hi, Marco."

Marco grins so big it looks more like excruciating pain than amusement.

"You're Wong," says Marco.

"I am Wong," says Cyril, nodding. "And stop smiling like that, man. It's creeping me out."

Now Jake knows. He keeps a wary eye on Marco, not-ing the odd twitches. Marco turns and looks directly at him, and the dark sheen over the big man's eyes is subtle but unmistakable.

"You're Viper," says Jake.

Lucas and Cyril stare at Jake, then at Marco.

Marco now looks pleased. But he doesn't speak.

"We sent your Clan away," says Jake. "Hunter gave us the abort code, and so they left."

Now a look of uncertainty passes over Marco's oily eyes.

"Is that so?" he says.

"Yes, that's so," says Jake.

"So you defeated me," says Viper. His smug look returns.

"Yes," says Jake. "So get out of our friend Marco. And then leave Carrolton. Go home." He takes a step toward Marco. "Never come back."

Marco's face twists into a hideous grin again.

"No, I like it here," he says.

Jake squints. "Why?" he asks.

"Because your species is so often *stupid* with fear," he says. "Your fear instinct makes you weak and easy to manipulate."

"You lost," says Jake. "It's over for you."

Through Marco, Viper barks a thick laugh. "I control a transnational organization," he says. "I control means that most nations on this planet would envy. I control things you wouldn't believe."

Jake nods. "Fear and control," he says. "Wow. Fun!"

Marco's eyes flare angrily.

"What a pathetic life you lead," adds Jake.

"Shut up, Bixby!" says Viper.

Jake can't help it: He laughs, somewhat harshly. "You sound like our local bully," he says.

Viper is livid now. He bares his teeth in a primal show of hatred. "Perhaps I can *demonstrate* the pleasures of fear and control, Bixby," he says in a low hiss. The huge man takes a step toward Jake now.

"Viper," calls a voice. A girl's voice: Lexi's voice, actually.

Marco spins to face the south door.

"Hunter," he says with undisguised loathing.

Hunter, in the form of Lexi, stands in the south doorway. She has a rucksack slung on her shoulder. She quickly slides it off and flings it to Lucas. Then she moves

168

lightly across the warehouse floor toward Viper/Marco.

They face off. Hunter slowly begins to circle Viper, who stays rooted in one spot.

"I've learned much since our last meeting," says Hunter, giggling girlishly.

Viper rubs his hair, but his hand gets stuck. "I will crush you," he says.

"This is unnatural," says Cyril. "*Come on*, you guys. You're cousins!"

Indeed, the sight of Lexi Lopez, all of four feet nine inches tall and weighing in at a hefty eighty-two pounds, squaring off against the six-foot-four-inch and two-hundred-forty-eight-pound Marco Rossi, looks very odd. Comical, even.

Suddenly, a car engine roars in the distance, then gets louder as it approaches. Jake turns to the main door, the direction of the sound. Outside, the vehicle squeals to a halt on the cracked asphalt. Two car doors open and then slam shut.

Halting footsteps approach.

"Unfortunately, that doesn't sound like the cavalry," mumbles Cyril.

Mr. Latimer appears in the main doorway, propping up a slumping Dr. Conrad. But then the gray-haired man pulls away and staggers straight toward Marco, pointing directly at him.

"Cast him out!" he shouts.

Marco eyes him disdainfully. "Dr. Conrad, I am through with you," he says.

"Listen to me, Marco!" cries Dr. Conrad. "You can force him out. I did it, several times. I was too weak to completely escape. But that's how I got my messages to these children. I forced Viper *out* of me. You can too!"

Marco drops to his knees. His face trembles.

"You will . . . *not*," he moans. Then he seizes his own hair, yanking it hard.

Suddenly, the sparkling nanoswarm rises from the warehouse floor, right next to Marco. It widens its spiral until it engulfs Marco, who starts coughing. His eyes swim in black oil.

"Yes," coughs Viper. "This will do."

Marco falls forward, hacking out mouthfuls of syrupy black fluid. The whirlwind seems to suck up the oil as fast as it falls. It flashes silver a few times, then transforms into a smoky black cloud of churning dust.

"Viper's in the swarm now!" cries Lucas.

"He'll get away!" cries Dr. Conrad.

But now Lexi the Hunter steps forward. Hands raised, palms turned out, she slowly approaches the black mist. The swarm churns slower. Individual strands freeze in midair like bits of black thread. Jake, watching this, remembers how The Kid did the same thing to the nanoswarm in the schoolyard, just a few hours ago.

Soon the mist no longer moves.

"Lucas Bixby!" calls Hunter. Her face strains with pure focus and concentration.

"Yes," answers Lucas.

"Open the chamber."

Lucas opens the rucksack and pulls out a remarkably light silver container about the size of a shoebox. He sees a small latch.

"Open it!" cries Hunter. "Hurry!"

Lucas presses the latch and the box lid slowly flips open. "Got it!" he says.

"Underneath him!" gasps Hunter.

Lucas scoots on his knees under the frozen black mist and slides the box underneath. Then, slowly, Lexi lowers her hands. The black strands begin to knit into a formless lump. They lower slowly, as well. Within half a minute or so they drop into the box. Lucas can see movement now. The black shape is wriggling—no doubt struggling to escape.

"I'm losing it," gasps Hunter. "Quickly!"

Lucas dives to the box and flips the latch. The lid snaps shut.

For a second there is utter silence.

Then Jake steps to the box. He looks at Lexi. "Would this be an antigravity containment chamber?" he asks.

Lexi just nods, clearly spent.

Lucas turns to Dr. Conrad. "This was your Omega Link message to us."

"Of course," says Dr. Conrad. "Viper is primarily a dark

matter entity. His atomic structure cannot be contained by normal baryonic matter—the stuff of the known universe. Only antigravitic force can *cage* him, as it were."

Lucas stares down at the sealed box, then at Lexi.

"Can he escape?" he asks.

"Yes," says Hunter. "But I will take him now, before he can find a way."

Suddenly, the Slorg bounds in through one of the west cargo doors.

"Well, the whole gang's here," says Cyril.

Lexi turns to the Slorg. "This creature is a good vessel for me," she says. She turns to Jake. "Good-bye, Jake Bixby."

Lexi abruptly falls to her hands and knees, hacking out mouthfuls of syrupy black fluid. After a few seconds she looks up with glazed eyes.

"Well, *that* was unpleasant," she says.

As Hunter quickly inhabits the black beast, Lucas gingerly picks up the containment chamber and slides it back into the rucksack.

Lexi stands unsteadily, looking at Lucas.

Lucas glances down at the rucksack . . . then hands it to Lexi.

She slings it gently around the Slorg's neck.

"Good-bye," she says sadly.

The Slorg meets her gaze with its fierce red eyes glazed with oily blackness. Then it turns and bounds off into the night.

(14)

THE FINAL CHAPTER

Hey, what's going on down there?

Look! Hundreds of people have gathered at a freeway on-ramp.

It looks suspicious. Let's check it out.

Zoom in, please.

This little-known ramp runs from the Klonsky Toll Road up onto the expressway as it passes over the north end of Carrolton. A blue Toyota Avalon sits by the curb at the base of the ramp.

All around the car, meat sizzles on gas barbecue grills. Man, that smells good. Long folding tables, covered with platters of food, line the street. Huge metal tubs of ice are chock-full of soda pop. Folks wander around with paper plates heaped with burgers and dogs and beans and potato salad and coleslaw and chips and pickles and you name it—if it's a common picnic item, it's on some-body's plate.

Somebody set up a bandstand too. Right now, a brass band plays the *Star Wars* theme. Awesome!

And look over there! Hey!

The four members of Team Spy Gear, fresh from saving the world yet again, sit unhappily on the curb next to the blue car. They watch people slap Mr. Latimer on the back and shake his hand or hug him. Many people have tears in their eyes as they bid farewell to Carrolton's favorite homeless guy.

"I don't like this," says Lexi. She's moping, big-time. "Why do things have to end?"

"We're supposed to be happy for him," says Lucas without much conviction. "After all, he *is* going home at last."

"*This* is his home," says Lexi.

Lucas nods. "Yes, but what about his family?"

"*We're* his family," she says.

Lucas has nothing to say to that. He just nods and looks over at his big brother.

Jake feels a bittersweet pang in his chest. He knows things are changing. Lately, he's found himself staring at familiar things, wondering how long they'll stay the same. Things he thought would *never* change, like the ancient, gnarly White oak tree in Platte Park, seem remarkably fragile to him now.

Jake spots Marco's dreadlocks dangling above the crowd.

"Yo, big man!" shouts Jake. "Over here!"

Marco emerges from the throng. With him is Dr. Conrad, looking much healthier than the last time they saw him, two weeks ago.

"Bixby," says Marco, nodding.

Jake nods back, then says, "You look great, Dr. Conrad."

"Thank you, Jake," he replies. "I'm half the man I used to be, but of course that's a good thing." He gets a kick out of his own joke.

Jake grins and says, "What's the word from the Agency?"

Marco raises his massive brows. "They've shut down Viper's operations worldwide . . . with ease, if you can believe them."

Dr. Conrad nods. "His network was paper-thin," he says. "Held together by his presence, as it were."

"By fear," says Jake.

"Exactly," nods Dr. Conrad.

Marco glances at Lexi, then around at the crowd. "Is, ah, your mother here?" he asks.

"Yes," says Lexi.

Marco stares at her. Lexi just grins.

"So?" he says.

"So . . . do you want to meet her?" asks Lexi.

"No," says Marco.

Lexi jumps up. "Come on," she says, grabbing his hand. "She's serving cake at the dessert table."

"Let go of my hand," says Marco as she drags him toward the bandstand.

The boys and Dr. Conrad watch them go.

"I have a question about the Hunter," says Lucas.

"Sure," says Dr. Conrad. He sits on the curb next to the boys. Looking around with a vague smile, he says, "You know, this really is a very pleasant town you have here."

"Thanks!" says Cyril. "I decorated it myself."

Lucas looks up at the gray-haired man. "What happened to Hunter? Do you know?"

Dr. Conrad shakes his head.

"What about that kid's body he was using?" asks Lucas. "I've been worried about that."

"No, no, that body wasn't human or even biological . . . not as we understand biology, anyway," says Dr. Conrad. "It was a synthetic life-form that served its purpose as a vessel well."

"Where is it now?" asks Lucas.

"Oh, we sent it to our Groom Lake facility," says Dr. Conrad.

"Ah, *Groom Lake*," says Cyril knowingly. "Of course. I'm sure they tossed it in the freezer with all the Roswell stuff."

"What's Groom Lake?" asks Jake.

Cyril looks stunned. "You've never heard of *Area 51*?" he says.

Jake glances around, trying to determine where that sudden blare of scary music is coming from. "No," he replies.

"It's where they keep all the [CENSORED BY THE UNITED STATES GOVERNMENT]," says Cyril.

Jake is horrified. "How could that be?"

"[JOKE CENSORED BY THE UNITED STATES GOVERNMENT]," says Cyril.

Jake laughs hysterically. It's the funniest joke he's ever heard. People for miles around start laughing. Even people who didn't hear it are laughing.

Dr. Conrad stares wistfully into space.

He says, "I spent five years of my life sitting next to a praying mantis."

Cyril nods thoughtfully. "Did he smell bad?"

"Yes," says Dr. Conrad. "And I'll never get those years back."

"What was the point of the bug?" asks Lucas.

"Fear, pure and simple," says Dr. Conrad. "Viper dealt with a lot of tough customers."

"But why a praying mantis, in particular?" asks Lucas.

"Ever seen a seven-foot mantis up close?" asks Dr. Conrad.

"No, thank God," says Lucas.

Dr. Conrad just shivers.

"So he used *you* as a 'vessel' to communicate, and he used the mantis to scare people," says Jake.

"Yes," says Dr. Conrad. "He really *enjoyed* scaring people."

Suddenly the crowd around the freeway ramp starts buzzing, and there is a flurry of movement. Jake stands up. So do the others. People are gathering around the blue Toyota Avalon.

"There he goes," says Jake. The bittersweet pang in his chest intensifies.

"Wow" is all Cyril can say.

Lucas just watches with wet eyes.

"Was he your friend?" asks Dr. Conrad.

"Yes, yes he was," says Jake.

Dr. Conrad nods. "Do you want to go say good-bye?" he asks.

"We already did," says Jake.

Earlier this morning, Mr. Latimer took Team Spy Gear on a car tour, following what he called his "patrol route" around Carrolton. It took hours; he couldn't drive more than one or two blocks at a time without neighbors running out with farewell gifts of rolls and coffee and photo albums full of memory shots. The tour got Mr. Latimer talking about old times . . . memories he would keep forever, he said. Afterward, he dropped off the team at Willow Park and they all said good-bye.

Lexi was so sad that Jake had to carry her piggyback for a few blocks.

Now Mr. Latimer, tears streaming down his cheeks, waves as his car accelerates up the on-ramp. He cruises past a sign that reads "Expressway South."

Soon the blue car is lost in the speeding flow of the southbound freeway.

People mingle and eat and listen to the music and talk and tell stories about Mr. Latimer for hours after he leaves.

Lucas and Lexi sit on the edge of the bandstand eating squares of cake.

"This cake is good," says Lucas, chomping.

"It makes me want to be a baker," says Lexi.

"I've already had, like, twelve pieces," says Lucas.

"Let's get more," says Lexi.

"I'm so with you on this," says Lucas, standing.

Cyril and Cat Horton stroll past them holding hands. Lucas gives Lexi a mischievous look.

"Hey, guys," calls Lucas. "Now that the party's over, maybe you should go somewhere and, like, *kiss!*" He and Lexi start laughing hysterically.

Cat squints at them. "Why don't *you?*" she retorts.

Lucas and Lexi look stricken.

"What?" says Lucas.

"You're seventh graders," says Cyril. "Technically, you could start dating."

Shocked, Lucas and Lexi turn to stare at each other. It's true! For several seconds, they gaze deeply into each other's eyes. Slowly, they reach out for each other.

"I . . . I love you . . . sweetheart," says Lucas in his breathiest voice.

"I love you too . . . moose nose," whispers Lexi.

And then they start laughing like brain-damaged hyenas.

"Hooooooo, ha-ha-ha!" howls Lucas as if in pain. *"Oh, oh my God! Oh, it hurts!"*

Wait. Maybe he *is* in pain, actually. That can happen in these situations.

Meanwhile, Lexi is howling so hard that a snot bubble emerges from her left nostril. When Lucas sees this, he laughs harder, so hard that small explosions blow his ears off the sides of his head.

Now Lexi can't even stand up. She sees the earless Lucas and collapses due to a medical condition known as "funny legs," which turns leg bones into rubberized stalks, sometimes for days at a time. The only way to reverse the process is to roll around on the ground laughing. When Lucas sees her collapse, guess what he does? That's right: *he laughs!* In fact, internal cellular combustion now triggers the hardest laugh of all, the Hoot of Death. When stricken by the Hoot of Death, a kid just turns directly into a chicken. Within seconds, Lexi turns into a chicken also.

Cyril looks down at the two chickens squawking loudly at his feet.

"Sorry," says Cyril. He tosses them a handful of feed. Hungrily, Lucas and Lexi peck the pellets.

Now Jake walks up with Barbie Bickle.

"Did you make another joke?" asks Jake, eyeing the chickens.

"I think so," says Cyril.

Jake nods. "Uh, what are you guys doing now?" he asks Cyril and Cat. "Any good plans?"

"Yes," replies Cat. "We're going to mosey around the neighborhood, wasting as much time as we possibly can."

"Oh, can we come too?" squawks Lucas, pecking and scratching.

"Yes!" clucks Lexi. *"We're lovebirds!"*

Lucas shrieks with laughter at this. Tears flow from Lexi's eyes too. They start whacking each other on the back, screaming with stupendous guffaws of hilarity. Lucas starts to melt. This makes Lexi howl with laughter. She melts too.

Cyril gazes sadly upon the melting chickens.

"We'd better go," he says.

Cat nods. She slips her hand into Cyril's.

Jake eyes this casual Hand-Holding Maneuver, paralyzed with ghastly fear. He slides his eyes sideways at Barbie. Barbie coolly raises her jasmine-scented hand and slips it through Jake's arm.

"Don't worry, Bixby," she says. "I wouldn't touch your disgusting hand with a ten-foot pole."

Cyril grins hugely at this. "Hey," he says. "That's good. I *like* that."

"New plan," says Cat. "Let's head up to Forty Mounds of Fun." This is the theme park up north. "It's a great place to wander aimlessly."

"Good plan!" says Cyril, nodding. "There's a couple rides

there I haven't thrown up on yet. I'd like to hit them all."

"How about ice cream downtown instead?" asks Jake.

"Dog, that's a good plan too," says Cyril.

"Wait," says Cat. "Here's a plan." She points down the sidewalk. "Let's just walk and see what happens."

Dude! Everyone loves *this* plan.

Now Jake Bixby gazes around at his friends, old and new. He thinks about all the Spy Gear adventures of the past year.

Are they over?

High school, he knows, will be an exciting adventure series. For example: He wants to make the freshman soccer team. *That* will be an adventure. Carrolton High's jazz bands are super-good—the best in the region, they say—and so his upcoming audition for the saxophone section will certainly test his adventure skills.

But Jake Bixby knows that whatever adventure awaits him, whatever calls next, he will go with good friends who just happen to be world-class spies.

Ha! Jake grins.

Yes, folks, it's *that* grin: the world-famous, eye-crinkling one. It's the one that says: "You win some, you lose some, but I really like my friends."

He reaches down, picks up the two melted chickens, and shakes them hard until they pop back into the shapes of Lucas and Lexi again. Then the six friends, four old ones and two new ones, begin to stroll away with no real plan and . . .

Oh, no! The satellite spycam view is pulling up and away.

Wait! I'm not ready to leave Carrolton!

Look, I *really* don't want to go back to the International Space Station just yet. But, as I've said before, I have no control over this phenomenon. I'm just the author.

Dang!

So back we go . . . up, up into the sky. Good-bye, Bixbys! See you, Cyril! *Adiós*, Lexi Lopez!

Hurry! Take a look around before we're too high up to see stuff.

Look over there, where Marco Rossi throws back his head and laughs as he talks to Marta Lopez, the woman who happens to be both Lexi's mom *and* his own mother's best girlhood friend. Wow, they're having fun. They're telling stories to each other and laughing a lot. Nothing is more fun than telling stories about people you love, and I mean *nothing*. Trust me. If there's one thing you learn from this highly educational Spy Gear Adventure series, I hope it's that.

And over there: See that big guy with the blond crew cut?

That's Brad.

Brad leans against a black BMW sedan. He wears

baggy jean shorts and a Carlos Santana T-shirt. His massive arms are folded like great pork shanks across his chest. His pale blue eyes survey the crowd.

Brad smiles.

As a group of laughing kids wanders past, he reaches into his car and pulls out a floppy-brimmed black hat. He plops the hat atop one small boy's head. The boy laughs and says "Hey, thanks, mister!"

Brad just nods.

Thirty minutes ago, Brad turned down a promotion to Senior Executive Dark Man.

He plans to sell life insurance instead.

Wow, we're really picking up speed now. Everything's getting small. We've risen almost into the cloud cover. Quick, take one last look around. Dr. Conrad is right: Carrolton is a *heck* of a place, isn't it? I'll miss it a lot. But the great thing about a place like Carrolton is that . . . it's always there.

Ah, clouds blur the camera's view now. But wait: Check out that car on the expressway. A blue Toyota Avalon heads north, approaching Carrolton's Willow Road off-ramp. Its right turn signal is blinking.

Will it exit?

Keep watching that blue car . . . and please let me know what happens.

THE END